LOST BETWEEN

LOST BETWEEN

Waterford City and County
Libraries

NEW ISLAND

LOST BETWEEN

First published in 2015
by New Island Books
16 Priory Hall Office Park
Stillorgan
County Dublin
Republic of Ireland

www.newisland.ie

PRINT ISBN: 978-1-84840-463-2
EPUB ISBN: 978-1-84840-464-9
MOBI ISBN: 978-1-84840-465-6

British Library Cataloguing Data.
A CIP catalogue record for this book is available from the British Library.

Typeset by JVR Creative India
Cover design by Mariel Deegan
Printed by Essentra

This volume is published with the support of the
Istituto Italiano di Cultura, Dublino,
Ministero degli Affari Esteri e della Cooperazione Internazionale.

New Island receives financial assistance from The Arts Council (*An Comhairle Ealaíon*), 70 Merrion Square, Dublin 2, Ireland.

10 9 8 7 6 5 4 3 2 1

Contents

The Italo-Irish Literature Exchange: A Context

The writer and past board member of the Irish Writers' Centre (IWC), Catherine Dunne, using her status as an acclaimed novelist in Italy, spearheaded an initiative in 2011 which led to an extensive cultural relationship between Ireland and Italy and their writers. Partnered with ònoma, the IWC's counterpart, and led by Federica Sgaggio (author and journalist), the Italo-Irish Literature Exchange (IILE) was born.

The purpose of the Italo-Irish Literature Exchange was to provide a forum for Italian and Irish writers to meet and to connect with each other by sharing and promoting their literatures in both countries. The IILE enables Irish and Italian writers to take part in readings, workshops, discussions, educational visits and other cultural events in both countries. The make-up of both the Irish and Italian groups was designed to showcase a mix of emergent and established writers in a range of genres, including novels, short stories, poetry, drama, screenplay, non-fiction and political satire.

There have been four visits to date under the IILE banner, two by Italian authors to Dublin (in 2011 and 2012), and two return visits by Irish authors to Verona (in 2012 and 2014). The latest exchange took place in June 2014; seven Irish novelists, playwrights and poets were selected from over sixty applicants by the Irish Writers' Centre to represent Ireland. The exchange began with a welcome reception and readings in the beautiful Villa Spada, home of the Irish embassy in Rome. The writers travelled south to the tiny town of Sant'Agata de' Goti (Campania) to meet the ònoma writers, where they jointly took part in educational and public events. The Irish writers then travelled to the Bologna area, where they met with members of the literary society and performed their work with a local poets' group, Gruppo 77. The tour received widespread press and media coverage, including a primetime slot on a national news channel.

The importance of place and identity played a major role in providing a template for the work produced for the 2014 exchange. Migration, and the role of writers and writing in response to the political and economic crises facing Italy and Ireland provided the raw material for the emerging stories and poems which are featured here in this volume. The sense of displacement described within these pages is, in effect, the universal glue that binds us together across cultures, and the writings reflect this theme.

Part of the ambition of this project is that the IILE is not just about the journeys and encounters in each other's countries, but that the participant writers' creative work reaches out to a wider audience over different platforms.

With this in mind, we have connected with publishers and are well underway with plans for two separate print publications: this one in English in partnership with New Island and a mirror publication in Italian in partnership with Guanda.

We consider these publications to be very important in the development of the IILE. They represent a current, permanent record of the creative work of the IILE writers, with the potential for inviting new international readers, writers and promoters to sample the best in contemporary writing and poetry in Ireland, Italy, and further afield.

It is important to acknowledge that all phases of the IILE were made possible with the kind support of our funding partners, the Arts Council of Ireland, Culture Ireland, the Istituto Italiano di Cultura – Dublino, the Irish Copyright and Licensing Agency and all of the donors of our Fund it campaign.

Valerie Bistany
Director, Irish Writers' Centre
7 April 2015

Foreword

When the two of us first met, back in 2010 at the Irish Writers' Centre in Dublin, it became clear very quickly that our initial friendship was about to expand and develop into a collaboration. We spent hours discussing the many cultural and traditional values shared by Ireland and Italy, including the love of storytelling.

Those early exchanges continued and, in 2011, the Board of the Irish Writers' Centre hosted a 'Cultural Conversation' between dozens of Italian and Irish readers and writers. The event was a resounding success and showed us that there was an appetite for closer literary ties between our two countries. There was also an opportunity to showcase the talents both of established *and* emerging writers in each of our countries; something that went to the very core of our philosophy. We were fortunate, too, to have the support and enthusiasm of the Italian Cultural Institute, in the form of the then director, Angela Tangianu, and of Sinéad Mac Aodha of the Ireland Literature Exchange.

And so, in 2012, seven established and emerging Irish writers travelled, with the financial assistance of Culture

Ireland, to Nogarole Rocca/Verona. We were hosted there by the Italian writers' group, ònoma, who had organised well-attended public events in a variety of locations. As in Dublin, audiences were keen to attend and to listen to writers reading their work in their mother tongue – and then to enjoy the experience of hearing that work translated into their own.

In 2013, it was the turn of the Italian writers – both emerging and established – to visit Dublin. For this second edition of the Italo-Irish Literature Exchange, we were honoured to have among us the internationally renowned Dacia Maraini. The public theatre of the Botanic Gardens was filled to capacity on that occasion and set the tone for yet another group of writers to meet and share their work with each other and with new audiences, this time in 2014 and, once again, in Italy.

Seven Irish writers met with their Italian counterparts in the mediaeval village of Sant'Agata de' Goti, close to Naples, and the cultural and writerly exchanges continued, with all concerned forming new links at both personal and institutional levels.

All writing is an act of translation – the translation of experience into words, into image and metaphor. The fifteen writers whose work forms this anthology take 'Displacement' as their theme. Their writing is a rich mix of poetry and prose, their approaches as diverse as the writers themselves. Their stories and poems are moving, insightful, and sometimes startling. The observations we find there are frequently offbeat, slyly humorous, and the joy of playing with language is everywhere evident.

'Displacement' is something familiar to both the Irish and Italians: emigration is a *leitmotif* of both of our histories. Both countries are recent democracies whose struggles for independence have had a profound effect on the shaping of their identities. Both nations have also traditionally emphasised the importance of family. Indeed, the sense of displacement within the family permeates many of these pieces, where family members are connected by their disconnectedness.

We see meditations on mortality – and writing – including William Wall's 'Grace's Day', where the enormous grief caused by the death of a child is experienced 'as a piece of fiction, less credible in fact because it had no internal order, no structuring principle'. In Giulio Mozzi's 'The Ship', the narrator reflects on how caring for his dying mother taught him that 'nothing disgusts me. I didn't know that before'.

Everywhere in this anthology we hear the authenticity of the writers' voices, voices that both give life to, and are given life by, the power of the imagination. Afric McGlinchey in 'Ghost of the Fisher Cat' speaks of the 'topography of our imaginations' that requires 'attention, a certain leap of your own/ to jump out of one world and into another'. Such a leap – where the boundaries between universes blur and shift, and the writer's use of language is our means of transport – is the focus of Fabio Viola's 'Amanita', where the narrator travels a road 'built of milk and marble' and where a village rests on an outcrop of rock, clinging there 'like the membrane between the toes of a webbed foot'.

The experience of alienation is also explored in these pieces – the sense human beings have of being disconnected from themselves and from others. The main character in Nuala Ní Chonchúir's slyly humorous 'Donor' is incapable of anything other than fleeting, sentimental attachments, and yet he reflects that a woman he meets has 'an ozone-sized hole in her psyche'. He may have a similar problem himself – but, as ever, lack of self-awareness can often go hand-in-hand with feelings of alienation. Similarly, in Gaja Cenciarelli's 'Bounded in a Nutshell', a doctor feels completely detached from her surroundings and from herself. She cannot even bear to touch her own body. A colleague observes that 'a woman like her would be out of place anywhere'. And in 'Calamities' by Ivano Porpora, the main character is rootless, aimless, stumbling from one self-induced crisis to the next. A stone shatters his window and he realises that, unlike him, the stone is 'perfect ... for the task assigned to it, after billions of years of being sanded down by water and the abrasions of wind'.

The relentless wash of history is also present in many of these pieces – either directly alluded to, or as a kind of bedrock that underlies our constant experience of change. In 'Statue Park', Noel Monahan looks on the statues of Lenin and the Communist Party, statues that were 'rounded up', uprooted from their important location on the streets, and are now gazed upon by 'tourists in Gucci sunglasses'. The statues are no more than symbols of a bygone era while around them the future gathers: 'New houses/Breathe' and 'night spills down the Danube'. In Seán Hardie's 'The

7

Count', which is an extract from a novel-in-progress, the eponymous hero is exiled to Ireland in 1972. He knows nothing about events in Ireland – but then he knows nothing about events in the rest of the world either. Not Bloody Sunday, not Watergate, not the Munich Olympics. Buried in his own privilege and sense of entitlement, the Count reflects that 'History comes, history goes, things change, nothing changes'.

The seventies also form the backdrop of Mia Gallagher's work-in-progress. It is 1976, and conflict in the North of Ireland is at its height. Violence is everywhere, coiled, ready to strike. The novel's male characters take refuge in the easy rhetoric of hatred, the bravado of political utterances after Guinness and whiskey: they taunt one of their number to '... show the Brits ... the fat cats ... the mohair suits in Kildare Street, show it as it is.'

Francesca Melandri's story 'Hong Kong Fishbowl' is rooted in that melting-pot of a city, in a bar where American soldiers lament the fact that they arrived too late to the war, the one 'they won but didn't fight in'. A character reminds them that 'some one hundred thousand people seem to have died...'

'Oh,' a young man replies 'those don't count... They were just soldiers.'

To write is also to be an outsider. The theme of 'Displacement' allows all of the fifteen writers, in their own unique way, to crawl into the skin of those who do not belong. In 'Liverpool/Lampedusa', Liz McManus explores the reality of enforced emigration, and the title reminds us of how ever-present the reality of that geographical displacement is today. The narrator speaks of Ireland post-Famine as that 'ill-fated country ... scourged by hunger and desolation'. There is a haunting resonance in the nineteenth-century emigrant overhearing tales of 'lives lost out on the Atlantic Ocean or the Mediterranean Sea: of boats wrecked in storms off the island of Lampedusa'. Things change, nothing changes.

Fabio Bussotti looks at the ways in which social identities are rapidly shifting. In 'Francesco' a teacher observes: 'I've got a class of twenty-two pupils. Six of them are of Chinese origin. Then I've got a Brazilian, a Vietnamese girl, four Moroccans and two Pakistanis. The rest are Italian... But really [...] Really, when you think about it, they're all Italians. They're all born here, in Rome.'

In 'Mother Tongue', Federica Sgaggio explores what it is to feel alienated from one's own language and culture. Even though the character is an outsider, she feels more at home in Ireland – a sanctuary after the end of a love affair and a pregnancy – than she does in her native Italy. *Self-satisfied shits,'* she thinks, observing some of her countrymen abroad. 'Ever since leaving Italy she could not abide their arrogant perfectionism.'

The antithesis of displacement, disconnectedness and alienation is, of course, love. It is through love that we find ourselves, and the other. In Gianpaolo Trevisi's fast-paced narrative, 'My Man and Me', love is redolent of homecoming, of belonging, a place where stars come to 'light up a thought, sliding on the silence'. A place where one is safe and feels whole. The lover here 'completes the other half of my own smile'.

Each story or poem is complete in itself, but together these pieces form a kaleidoscope of contemporary society; they look at how we navigate the spaces between the imagination and the mundane realities of our daily lives; they look at the contours of geographical displacement and the pain of emotional and physical loss. They confront suffering and grief, denial and death – the ultimate displacement – and they do so with energy, with passion, and with empathy.

We feel privileged to have been part of an initiative which has resulted in an anthology such as this – a unique venture, we believe, and we celebrate the fact that the collection will be published in both Ireland and Italy in 2015.

Thank you to all our contributors, and to our translator, without whom none of this would have been possible.

Catherine Dunne
Federica Sgaggio
June 2015

Dublin, November 1976
Mia Gallagher

Oh, she said, the first time they did it, staring up at his prints on the washing lines. You take photographs.

And?

Just. That's not what I thought.

He went quiet, as if she'd offended him, but she didn't care enough to ask why. Later, when they were fucking again, he brought it up. So what did you think I did?

Oh. A— it sounded stupid. I call you the Poet.

He laughed. Poet.

Sorry.

No. Say it...'

Sorry?

Say it to me.

I. Poet?

No. Like you mean it. Like it's my name.

Oh— she rolled her eyes, arched her back. Poet? Oh. Poet. Oh—

File, he said. It's an Irish word, for bard. Then he laughed again, at some private joke.

She wanted to tell him not to get carried away, she'd meant it ironically, but his eyes were closed and it would have felt unkind to put him straight. That surprised her: her unwillingness to wound, still there after everything.

Always the bleeding heart, Lotte.

She didn't ask him about his work; if it was work, not just a hobby. The sight of his prints strung overhead made her itch, yearn to get away. Can't you put those somewhere else? she'd asked instead, rather rudely. I can't stand the stink. The next time she came up, he'd obliged. Once he forgot and she hadn't had enough to drink and while he was busy down below, lapping away, she found herself sucked in. Analysing them, the old, critical cogs beginning to whirr again. They seemed promising, she'd thought, if a little haphazard; too grimy for a professional, not news enough for a hack. He'd taken a series of portraits: young boys riding ponies on a scrap of grey grass near a tower block. Their posture was defiant, but he'd found their eyes and made his way in, exposing their souls, their small fears and hopes, to anyone who might see.

Care you must take, Lotte. Don't let him turn that knack on you.

The second night, she noticed books littering his flat; compact, explosive conversation pieces. After that she made sure to get hammered before going up and, once in, scattered her clothes over everything that might have meaning for her, blotting out the familiar names, familiar titles. Marx, Trotsky, Marcuse—

Best not register the contents of his life. Best not let him register the contents of hers.

He calls her Evans. *Lottee, Lottay, that's too much work. I'll use your surname.* Funny, how a Welsh name had dissolved her perceived imperiality, like glue in rain. She didn't tell him the name wasn't hers, but the Captain's.

She hasn't told him anything; he hasn't asked. They don't talk about things.

Except for last night. She has the distinct, uneasy impression that last night they did a lot of talking.

He'd knocked on her door around seven, all dressed up: scarf and hat, duffel coat. He looked different. Boyish. Something shining in his eyes that wasn't just the drink.

Uh oh, she'd thought.

Ready?

She didn't say *For what.* Just leant against the wall and blew smoke into his face. He shrugged, irritated. Get your coat.

She should have laughed, slammed the door in his face. But it was cold and she hadn't the fire lit and – let's face it – she was lonely. While she dressed she made him wait in the hall; her gentleman caller, leashed to the other side of the threshold. She didn't want him nosing through her slowly filling bookshelves, the splashes of colour on her clothes rack, the few scraps of something beginning to populate her bare white space.

He'd nodded when he'd seen her, pleased. She'd made an effort. Crochet cap, fur-trimmed coat, new boots.

Outside, it had been on the edge of freezing, sharp and cold.

I love this time of year, she nearly said, but caught herself. Where are you taking me?

To hear some music.

What sort?

Ah ... his hands waved, vague. Irish.

They took a bus from Ballsbridge and went along the coast, down the grand leafy streets and onto the beach road, past the bird sanctuary and the outdoor baths, up around the port and the coves, right to the terminus; a pretty little village with winding streets.

Dalkey, said the Poet. It's famous. A famous writer lives here.

I didn't know you could read, she said, only half-teasing. He flushed, then laughed.

She'd felt alright on the journey, giggly, a little schoolgirlish, and it seemed odd but not wrong to hold hands and lean against him on the front seat, swaying as the bus rounded corners, allowing gravity to push them together, pull them apart. She'd caught sight of their reflection in the bus window and even thought, My God, how innocent. But once they got to the pub, a dingy basement full of smoke and the smell of Guinness, where a band in woollen jumpers were setting up in a corner, it changed. She began to feel hemmed in, more so when she realised he was meeting friends – all male, all young, bearded like relics from a more idealistic time. She didn't want his friends in her life. Especially not these, with their Gaelic names and their laughter when she failed to pronounce them correctly. She felt like leaving, returning to Baggot Street and Caliban, to — *home*. That surprised her — but then the Poet handed her a pint of Guinness and a whiskey chaser — I'd have got you a sherry if you weren't such a Women's Libber — and although it was a bizarre thing for him to say, an awful joke, if even that, she could feel the awkwardness behind it, the need to please, so she decided, against her wiser instincts, to stay.

What's it like now you're working for the enemy, Eoin? asked one of the friends. A Dubliner with close-set eyes and a bushy moustache.

The Poet glanced at her. Jesus, Christy, just—

Working? she thought. Odd that, not *enemy* but *working*.

Leave him be, Christy, said another man. Dark, self-contained, with a Northern Irish accent.

What do *you* think of that? The moustached one — Christy — was staring at her.

Sorry?

Eoin taking pictures for the Brits.

Confused, she looked at the Poet.

It's not the Brits, said the Poet. It's—

The Organ of the Liberal Bourgeoisie. Christy's words were enunciated too clearly, like an English person speaking school French. He laughed. Irish. Times. Irish? That's a right fucking joke.

The Irish Times, she thought. The newspaper?

That's stickie talk there, Christy, said the dark man.

Christy ignored him, kept staring at Lotte. I'm just asking Eoin what happened to his principles. *Tiocfaidh ár lá.*

Evans is Welsh, said the Poet.

Oh aye? said the dark one.

Still a left-footer, said Christy. Still a Subject of the bleeding Crown.

File. The Irish for bard. The Gaelic bards, he'd told her, had two roles: to flatter the power and, if crossed, to satirise it. Since when had he been working for a newspaper?

Actually, she heard herself say, I'm not Welsh. The Poet's head jerked towards her. I'm from Bristol. A — what's that word, Poet? — *Sasanach.*

Christy snorted into his pint.

Interesting city, Bristol. Hometown of Strongbow, I believe. She lifted her glass. Without whom my Saxon forbears would never have invaded this lovely little island of yours. *Sláinte.*

A collective intake of breath. Funny: nobody corrected her, said *It was the Normans, not the Saxons.*

Jesus, Evans, said the Poet. Just—

How long had he been working there?

Oh, don't get your knickers into a twist, Poet, she said, exaggerating the glottal stops she'd picked up in London. I'm not a proper English. No more than Christy here knows the least fucking thing about revolution.

Something brutish coiled in Christy's shoulders. Ah, she thought, it's coming, and that dead part of her wouldn't have been disappointed if he'd hit her. But instead the dark man laughed, revealing strong white teeth.

Lotte? he said. *Deutsch, oder?*

Christy looked puzzled.

Rote Armee Faktion, said the Northerner.

Fraktion, Du Idiot, she almost said, but the Poet interrupted. Jesus, quiet, will ye, the music's starting.

She could see the anger flickering in his face, and underneath it something raw and uncertain, but that was a fucking liberty, because if anyone deserved to be angry, it was her, and then the music began and people hushed, and even Christy lost interest in her and began enthusiastically thumping the back of the man beside him, and she drank the Guinness and the next chaser the Poet gave her, avoiding his eyes, and the next pint and chaser after that, and gathered, without really listening, that the Poet's friends, apart from the Northerner, were boys he'd met in the wild, dead years after he'd left school, three times he'd failed to get into Art College, too thick to get the message, too bloody-minded, too full of notions of his own genius, kept pestering the newspapers though, and now an uncle who was a subbie had pulled some strings, and she had only herself to blame, she'd seen the books, what had she thought she was playing at, to put her head in the lion's den like that? And they all drank another round, and somebody said how hot the weather would be in Belfast and they laughed, and slapped the Poet on his back, and told him, Now, Eoin, you show the Brits, you show the fat cats, you show the mohair suits in Kildare Street, show it as it is, Eoin, show everyone on this poxy island what's going on, those Orange pricks with their property and profits and proletariat-fooling lodges and no Catholics need apply, those B-Special bollixes, those trigger-happy para bastards, those warmongering imperial fuckers in Whitehall, those murdering cunts, you show them what the martyrs of 1916 died for, what the people on the streets of Derry were gunned down for. *You name it as it is*, shouted the Northern man, anointing the Poet's brow with whiskey, *for you are Eoin Báiste, John the Baptist! Eoin the Marxist!* shouted Christy, *Blessed Eoin!* yelled another, and she thought of the music he played when they fucked, the soundtrack to their rocking and rolling: his blues and Chuck Berry and Bowie and Velvet Underground and the weirder, brasher sounds with screeching guitars and voices yowling anarchy that belonged to some new thing called punk, and wondered what on earth that had to do with this, these fiddles and drums, these beards and oily jumpers, and what Belfast had to do with him or anything, especially her.

This is an edited extract from a novel, Beautiful Pictures of the Lost Homeland, *the development of which has been kindly supported by the Arts Council of Ireland and a residency with IADT/dlr Arts Office.*

Mia Gallagher writes short stories, novels and plays. Her award-winning short fiction has been published in Ireland and internationally, and her debut novel *HellFire* (Penguin, 2006) garnered wide critical acclaim and received the *Irish Tatler* Literature Award (2007). Extracts from *Beautiful Pictures of the Lost Homeland* have previously been published in the UK (OUP), the US and Ireland. Mia has received several Arts Council of Ireland bursaries for literature, two Arts Council playwriting grants and in 2009/10 was Writer in Residence with IADT/dlr Arts Office (Dun Laoghaire).

Francesco

Fabio Bussotti

When I ran up the steps of the Di Donato elementary school on Via Bixio, accompanied by Officer Emiliana Saggioro, it was about eleven o'clock in the morning. Only three hours had passed since my quiet reawakening after a night of strangely unbroken sleep. I'd come out of the house all dressed up and ready to go, washed and shaved, happy to enjoy the sunny springtime, the brilliant green of the plane tree leaves, the scent of cyclamens clinging to the art deco villas on Via Luzzatti. In leisurely style, I'd made my way to my office in the police station on Via Petrarca, pausing only to drink my usual coffee in my usual bar. Such an excess of unwarranted good cheer called for punishment, and so, bang on cue, here came the phone call.

'Francesco Xuong, a Chinese kid from class 5D, has run away from school. His teacher, Lucia, couldn't hold him back. The cleaning lady, Alfonsina, tried to intercept him, but she fell down the stairs and seems to have broken her hip...'

Officer Emiliana Saggioro was the one who took the call, and as she too was the mother of a child called Francesco, she leapt to her feet. 'We're on our way!'

The long high-ceilinged corridor on the second floor made a perfect sounding-board for the howls of despair coming from Lucia, the teacher. 'I tried to grab him, but he slipped through my fingers... He was shouting, kicking...'

Half a dozen fellow-teachers and two cleaning ladies with undamaged hips were huddled around Lucia, trying in vain to calm her down.

'Go around to his mother's place! The shop!'

Officer Saggioro joined the other women. '*Signora*, don't worry, we've already sent a car to his mother's shop.'

'Oh, please! I beg you!'

Behind the closed doors of the classrooms, you could almost hear the breathing of the children, like scared chicks waiting for the storm to pass.

I found a gap in the scrum and caught both of Lucia's hands in mine. The teacher's hands were cold, and damp with sweat. The veins in her wrists were rapidly pulsating. '*Signora*, I'm Flavio Bertone, the superintendent at the Esquilino station. Take it easy. We're going to find the boy.'

A cleaning lady brought a glass of water. I let go of Lucia's hands. Without once looking me in the eye, she raised the glass to her lips. She was shivering.

From the second-floor windows, the ambulance in front of the school gate was clearly visible. Three paramedics had loaded Alfonsina, the cleaning lady, onto a stretcher and, with considerable effort, were hoisting her on board the vehicle. This was a tough job because Alfonsina was a woman of rather sturdy build. I gestured to Officer Saggioro, to let her know we had to regain control of the situation. 'Please, ladies, all of you, kindly return to your classes. Is there a room where we could have a word with your colleague Lucia?'

We went down the stairs to the ground floor with one of the cleaning ladies leading the way, muttering and grumbling to herself. Officer Saggioro was holding Lucia by the arm; the teacher had stopped wailing, but was still in tears.

We came into a deserted classroom with four desks in the middle, surrounded by six or seven chairs, two cupboards with broken doors and a photocopying machine that had been dead for some time and was now buried in a corner. The cleaning lady muttered something and then left us alone. Officer Saggioro and Lucia were sitting side by side. I squatted opposite them on a chair so low that I could feel my knees brushing my chin.

'Now, Lucia, what can you tell me about this kid?'

Lucia blew her nose on a scrap of toilet paper that she held in her fist. She gave a big sigh and, for the first time, her eyes met mine. I could see just how she felt, with the full responsibility for that runaway child weighing on her shoulders. She was ashamed of her failure to stop Francesco. She wished she could die. And all this for less than thirteen hundred euros a month.

'Well, Mr Bertone, as you can see, this is a multi-ethnic school. We've got kids from all over the world...'

'I know, Lucia. Officer Emiliana Saggioro and myself, we live and work here in the Esquilino area...'

I had called her by her name, Lucia, in an effort to switch over to a friendly, informal atmosphere. It seemed to me she wasn't shaking quite so much now.

'I've got a class of twenty-two pupils. Six of them are of Chinese origin. Then I've got a Brazilian, a Vietnamese girl, four Moroccans and two Pakistanis. The rest are Italian... But really...'

Lucia paused for a moment. I thought I could detect an imperceptible smile on her lips. She looked straight at me with her damp brown eyes. She was a fine-looking woman. A forty-year-old giving her all to Mission Impossible for barely the minimum wage.

'Really, when you think about it, they're all Italians. They're all born here, in Rome.'

Saggioro patted her on the shoulder. 'And Francesco Xuong?'

'Francesco is a real problem-child. He often gets anger attacks. It takes two or three people to hold him down... We've asked for extra support, but they won't give us any because the money isn't there. His father has a drink problem, he was probably beating the mother... Now he's gone home to China. Francesco's mum is still here, on her own. She runs a clothes shop on Via Conte Verde, but she has her problems, and she can't control the boy's outbursts. They're happening on a daily basis now. Francesco had some traumas in early childhood...'

I stood up. I was tired of having my chin resting on my knees. 'Tell me about these outbursts of Francesco's.'

Lucia sighed, once again clasping her hand against her forehead. 'Anything at all can set it off. A tiny rebuke, something a classmate said, an assignment that's a bit too hard, a touch of exhaustion during the last hour of the day... He flies off the handle: suddenly, with no warning, he starts shouting curses, bad language or yelling "*I hate you!*" The veins on his neck swell up, he goes all red, he kicks and punches everyone... Once, two months ago, he even tried to throw himself out the window. God, we were terrified...'

As Lucia buried her head in her hands, my mobile phone vibrated. It was Inspector Pizzo. 'Superintendent? Good morning, sir. We're here with the boy's mother, in her shop. No, he's not here. No sign of him. His mother, though, doesn't seem too bothered. Apparently this is not the first time. Now she's phoning other relations who have shops in the district. There's an uncle who runs an accessories shop in Via Principe Eugenio, and a cousin of his father who sells straw hats near the Arch of Saint Vitus. But none of them has seen Francesco.'

'What about home?'

'They live in Via Principe Amedeo, number 19, second floor, but there's nobody in, and Francesco doesn't have a key...'

'Okay, thanks, we'll talk again.'

Lucia had stood up. Eyes wide. 'Any news?'

'Not yet, but we're searching everywhere. We'll soon find him.'

'My God...' She was about to break into tears again. Officer Saggioro put her arm around her shoulders and gave her a squeeze. 'Don't worry, it'll all work out.'

'Yes, Lucia, don't worry. And when you feel up to it, do go back to your class. The other kids definitely need you there. Emiliana Saggioro will stay here in the school, to cope with whatever happens. Francesco might even decide to come back to class.'

Lucia murmured her thanks, almost inaudibly. I took her hands in mine again. They were clammy. I would have liked to put my arms around her, but police superintendents are not allowed to go into schools and hug teachers who are having a rough day.

I left the school building and turned into Via Conte Verde. In the distance, I recognised Inspector Pizzo by his big nose. He was standing beside a Chinese woman who was talking into her mobile phone. This was Francesco's mother, and she was alerting the whole Chinese community to what had happened. Without a doubt, this was the best way of finding the child. And as they had no need of me, I walked on quickly and made my way towards Via Principe Amedeo, number 19.

The main door of the apartment block, built in the late nineteenth century, was flanked on one side by an Indian restaurant and on the other by a money transfer shop. The area was filled with the strong smell of onions and curry. The garbage bins out front were overflowing with empty fruit trays. From an overturned bag, crab claws had slithered out, covering the footpath. Some passers-by were stamping on them to hear them crunch underfoot.

I went into the courtyard and raised my eyes towards the display of coloured cloth spread out to dry. Smells and noises seemed to have faded away. Three bicycles were fastened to the downpipe from the gutter, secured by a heavy chain. A weeping fig tree, about two metres high, provided a welcoming ornament together with four pots of geraniums lined up beside the elevator door. At the top of the first flight of stairs sat a solitary girl, about ten years of age. Dark hair, dark eyes. She might have been Indian or Pakistani. I went over to the stairs and called up to her. 'Hi, my name is Flavio and I'm a police superintendent. What's your name?'

'Urbi.'

'What age are you?'

'Ten.'

I'd got that right. 'Where are you from?'

She replied with a look of amazement. 'From here. From Piazza Vittorio. Why?'

I had asked a stupid question. I thought again about what Lucia had said about the kids in her class, born in Italy. 'No, what I meant to say was ... Your family, where did they come from?'

'They're from Bangladesh, but I was born here.'

'Why are you not at school?'

Urbi lowered her eyes. A shadow of sadness was clouding her face.

'Tomorrow we're off to London. We're moving there.'

'Why's that?'

'My dad says there's no more work to be had here in Italy.'

'What's your dad's job?'

'Cook.'

'Where do you go to school?'

'Di Donato School.'

'Are you sad to be leaving your classmates?'

Urbi looked at me again in amazement, as if to ask, Are you completely stupid? What kind of question is that? Then she nodded.

'Listen, Urbi, do you know a boy the same age as yourself, who lives here, in this apartment block, called Francesco?'

Urbi nodded again.

'When was the last time you saw him?'

'This morning.'

'Early this morning, when he was on his way to school?'

'No, this morning. Just a short while ago.'

'What does that mean?'

Urbi looked up with her dark, intelligent eyes. She was calculating the time. 'Oh ... Half an hour ago.'

'And where did you see him?'

'In the courtyard.'

'And what was he doing?'

'Running. When he saw me, he said "*Shhhh!*", and put a finger to his lips.'

'And then?'

'I don't know, I think he went and hid.'

'Here, in the apartment block?'

Urbi shook her head. The answer was no.

'Where, then?'

'Outside.'

'Where do you mean, outside?'

This was a delicate moment. I was doing my best to remain calm and smiling, but I knew it was possible that the girl was playing games with me.

'Where everything's a mess.'

'What do you mean?'

'Where everything's a complete mess, it's easier to hide.'

Urbi was testing me, there was no doubt about that. If I were really a policeman as I claimed, I would know how to respond. I thought about it, for a few moments, while those big eyes looked me up and down.

'Where everything's a mess: you mean the place where everything's all over the shop… The market, then!'

Urbi smiled. And I smiled with her. 'So, Francesco could be there.'

'That's what I think, yes.'

I should have rushed across the street, into the throngs of the Piazza Vittorio market, looking for Francesco, but I didn't want to leave Urbi like that, without wishing her the very best of luck for her new life in London. 'Are you scared of this move to England?'

'No.'

'You'll have some problems with the language…'

She stopped me at once. 'No, we all speak English.'

'Have you got brothers and sisters?'

'Two. One brother, one sister.'

'Older than you?'

'No, younger.'

I smiled at her. 'All the best, then.'

'You too.'

I left her there, sitting all alone on the stairs. Before leaving the courtyard, I turned again to wave goodbye.

In the Piazza Vittorio market, everything, as Urbi had said, was a complete mess. The world population of the Esquilino district does its shopping every day among those stalls that provide clear proof of globalisation in the farm and food sectors. I thought – wrong as usual – the best thing to do would be to go and look among the Chinese market stalls. There are three of them, practically identical. What they have on display is bunches of pak choi, bitter in the mouth and with a peppery aftertaste; frozen shellfish and prawns, extra-long runner beans with impossible names, sweet-and-sour sauces, bean sprouts, crisp white cabbage and frozen fruit. The usual products were all there, plain to see, but none of the market sellers had seen Francesco Xuong passing by.

The Pakistani vegetable sellers called me 'Chief' or 'Handsome'; they were very anxious to sell me flavourless courgettes at less than one euro a kilo. I wasn't looking for courgettes, I was looking for an Italian child of Chinese origin called Francesco.

When I came to Antonio, the Italian butcher at stand 74, I asked if he had seen a ten-year-old Chinese kid. He replied that he hadn't seen any Chinese kids, but could offer me new grilled lamb skewers from Avezzano that in his opinion were out of this world. 'Mister, these are the business.'

I got away from Antonio's lamb skewers and made straight for the Hungarian meat stall, where I often bought a few hundred grams of a delicious smoked sausage with an aftertaste of cumin.

Sadly, the Hungarians hadn't seen Francesco either.

Adelina, the lady who I bought white eggs laid by Leghorns from, said she had seen a Chinese kid passing her stall and making for the fish counters. 'I know him well, mister, he's called Francesco, he lives just over there on the Via Principe Amedeo…'

I crossed the aisle with the fish counters, where an Indian with a pirate beard wanted to sell me a real octopus of enormous dimensions. I turned left into the spice aisle, and stopped in front of Mario's stall. Mario, from Sri Lanka, is the man I always go to for my hot paprika. In front of his stall was an enormous pyramid of bitter gherkins, long and knobbly, much loved in the Near and Far East. Francesco was right there, at the foot of the gherkin pyramid. He crouched there, frightened; he could barely keep his eyes open. I leaned down towards him. 'Hi, my name is Flavio. I'm a cop, I'm friends with your mother and your teacher. If you don't mind, we'll go back to school. We'll say sorry to Miss Lucia, your teacher, and we'll say sorry to your classmates, and then we'll tell your mum you're okay and you'll never do this sort of thing again. Give me your hand.'

Francesco was worn out. His eyes were blank. He seemed completely without strength. A pale, bloodless little bird. In spite of all that, he stretched out his hand to me. No hesitation. We were old friends already. I was looking for him and he was waiting for me. As if everything were already laid down: all we had to do was go back to school. Hand in hand.

*

One month after his runaway day, Francesco still has his moments of madness. Not every day, but at least three times a week. His mother, the teachers and the school principal don't know how to cope. What they need is a support teacher, a paediatric neuropsychiatrist who knows how to deal with these cases, but there's no money for things like that, and no one wants to take the responsibility.

Unfortunately, I'm only a simple police superintendent. I do what I can. Officer Saggioro has given me a phone number for Lucia, the teacher. I call her frequently to have a little chat about Francesco, and the problems facing a school and a city district full of migrants. Tomorrow we're going to meet, Lucia and me, and look in one another's eyes.

Translated from the Italian by Cormac Ó Cuilleanáin.

Fabio Bussotti was born in 1963. He is a cinema, TV and theatre actor. He worked with directors like Gassman, Fellini, Olmi and Monicelli. In 1989 he won the Nastro D'Argento prize for the film *Francesco* by Liliana Cavani. As a novelist, he debuted with the thriller *The Envy of Velázquez* (Sironi, 2008), translated in Russia and Spain. In 2012 he published *The Waiter of Borges* (Perdisa Pop), receiving unanimous approval from critics and readers. His latest spy story is *Borromini's Tears* (March 2015, Mincione Edizioni).

The Count

Sean Hardie

The young Count Rudolph was unusually tall and thin, like a grasshopper in steel-rimmed glasses. He lived with his father, the Old Count, his mother, his younger brother Wolf and their tutor in a castle in Bavaria. At least, it was called a castle – Schloss Bernenberg – although it was really more of a small château or a large manor house. Yellow and white and blue, with tall windows and decorative turrets, it was rimmed by immaculate gardens and a park planted with ancient oaks where spotless cows grazed among the deer. There was an ornamental lake, a walled kitchen garden, dovecots, a dog cemetery with marble headstones and a romantic woodland walk leading to a Greek folly. Peacocks and guinea fowl wandered the lawns. The gravel was raked every week. No weed would dare grow in the rose beds. The sound of gardeners at work ticked like a clock in the distance. Beyond the park lay forests, meadows and a vineyard.

The tutor's name was Carl Joseph, a fat, neat little man with a high girlish voice and a paralysing fear of the numerous decorative hunting dogs which patrolled the Schloss and its grounds. His job was to ensure his pupils knew what they needed to know. There were correct and incorrect ways of doing everything – declining Greek verbs, laying out a genealogical table, calculating the earth's gravitational pull. At eight years old, Rudolph already knew them by heart. At Sunday lunch, for example: quenelles, rissoles and patties should be eaten with a fork; salad on a side plate with a knife and fork. But cucumber should be eaten on the dinner plate, also with a fork. Pastry too should be eaten with a fork. In the case of a fruit tart, however, a dessert spoon should be used as well as a fork, but only for the purpose of conveying the fruit and juice, not the pastry, to the mouth. In the case of stone fruit – cherries, damsons, plums, etc. – either the dessert spoon or the fork should be raised to the lips to receive the stones, which should be placed to the side of the plate; but when the fruit stones are of larger size, they should be separated from the fruit with the fork and spoon and left on the plate, and not put into the mouth. Jellies and blancmanges should also be eaten with a fork.

Rudolph's brother Wolf was a miniature of his father. He knew how to give orders to servants and lectures to strangers who strayed onto the estate. When Rudolph came across strangers he hid, lay on his stomach in the bushes and wondered what it would be like to be someone from the outside world. Wolf knew how to play with other children; Rudolph did not. Whenever possible, he retreated to the attics, to the room at the end which he had set up as a factory for the manufacture of miniature soldiers, melting down small tablets of tin over a Bunsen burner, pouring the molten metal into moulds to produce inch-high dragoons and cavalry men, which he laid out in lines on the floor. Whole regiments of them, with flags and standards and gun carriages and coaches drawn by stallions to carry generals and royalty and general staff – exactly as they were deployed on the eve of Frederick the Great's victory over the Austrians at Rossbach in 1757.

The morning after the incident with young Greta, the old Count telephoned his diplomat cousin in Dublin and instructed him to find a house for his son, somewhere not too big and not too small, preferably remote, perhaps with some woodland for hunting.

Early November, 1972. Rudolph is twenty-three years old. He has never left Germany before; he knows no one in Ireland. A cold north wind scutters the clouds across the thin blue sky over the long ridge of the Blackstairs Mountains. Rudolph sits in the back of a five-year-old brown Toyota with a dented wing and the letter T missing from the Taxi sign on its roof, heading south. Irish towns all look the same to him. Unwashed, untidy, unloved; long streets of drab little shops, drab bars, rusted tin-roofed petrol stations, ugly Our Lady grottos with the blue paint peeling outside ugly concrete churches, unwashed cars, litter everywhere.

They follow a tractor into another small, anonymous town. Rudolph sees a hotel sign. He speaks for the first time since they left the airport, tells the driver it's lunchtime. The taxi pulls over. They both get out. The driver leans against the bonnet of the Toyota and lights a cigarette. Rudolph goes into the hotel. The dining room is empty and unheated, chocolate-brown walls, an orange carpet with black and red swirls, a smell of damp and tobacco smoke and boiled cabbage. Half a dozen tables have been laid with cutlery and tea cups and cruets and bottles of brown sauce. He sits down and waits. No one comes. He coughs. Nothing happens. After five minutes, a boy carrying a box of root vegetables passes through on his way to the kitchen.

'Excuse me,' says Rudolph.

The boy stops and looks at him blankly.

'I would like to order lunch.'

'Lunch.'

'Lunch.'

'I'll see if I can find her.'

He vanishes, leaving the box of vegetables on a chair. Rudolph studies the room in more detail. A tarnished mirror, a poster of a fat man in a cowboy hat holding a guitar, Big Tex O'Neill and the Lowdowners, appearing two months previously at Doran's. A small vase of plastic flowers.

A woman in an apron appears.

'Grand day,' she says. She hands him a single-sheet menu. Rudolph puts on his glasses. Soup, chicken or gammon or cod.

'What's in the soup?'

'Vegetables.'

'Soup, please. And chicken.'

'Would you like tea with that?'

'Tea? No thank you.'

The soup is a strange grey colour with lumps of something white that might be turnip. He leaves it untouched but manages a little of the chicken.

They drive on south. Ash trees, sycamore, rowan, tattered hedgerows, dry stone walls. Improvised gates made from pallets and bedsteads. An ancient Morris van with no wheels abandoned in a field of rushes. In another field, three small black cows drink from an old bath. Brambles. Cattle. Crows, everywhere crows. A landscape like an old sofa with the stuffing coming out. Ivy. More crows. Low hills rising to a bare ridge. The sun is disappearing behind the hills by the time they reach the valley and arrive at a narrow bridge over a wide, peat-brown river. The driver asks Rudolph if he knows the way from here. Rudolph opens his briefcase, takes out an Ordinance Survey map, leans forward and points with a gloved finger.

'A mile up the hill, a small turn to the right, a little road drops back down to the river, after another mile and a half we will find the gates.'

He puts the map back in his briefcase, closes the clasp. They drive past the gates without noticing them. The road climbs away from the river up a steep hill. There is grass in the middle now, potholes you could farm fish in. Rudolph gets the map out again. They turn round and head back down, discover the gates, which are buried in ivy and blackthorn. A dark narrow gap between the laurel and rhododendron bushes leads to a gothic nave of monkey puzzles and cedars.

The house is gloomy, Edwardian, larger than he expects. It's surrounded on three sides by trees, with outbuildings and a stable yard at the back. To the front, the outline of a lawn is still just visible amongst the hog weed and brambles. At home it might have belonged to – no, no one at home would let a house rot like this. He stands, polishing his spectacles with the corner of his handkerchief while the driver takes his suitcases out of the boot and carries them up the steps. The fare has been prepaid by his father's cousin. The driver puts the cases down, waits. Rudolph realises he wants a tip. He has no idea how much to give him.

'How much?'

'It's up to yourself.'

'How much is normal?'

The driver smiles.

'I'd say upwards of a hundred.'

Rudolph gets out his wallet, starts counting out notes. The driver watches him until he's finished.

'I'm joking. Give me a fiver.'

He takes the money, shakes Rudolph's hand, gets back in the car and disappears down the drive. Rudolph is alone. A cat has left a dead jackdaw beside the boot scraper.

It's country quiet. A tractor somewhere down in the valley. Rooks argue in the sycamores, somewhere in the yard water splatters from a blocked gutter. Further off, beyond the trees, the cloud creeps down the mountain towards the bog. He feels as though he's surrounded by a vast wet animal.

He folds his handkerchief and puts it back in his pocket, takes out his key, unlocks the door and goes inside. The previous owner died heirless, and the house comes as he left it: sold off by the estate, lock, stock and teaspoons. It's clean, a smell of dogs and mildew and disuse overlaid with disinfectant and wax polish. A stone-flagged hall with an umbrella stand and boot rack gives way to three reception rooms with high sash windows hung with thick sagging curtains, furnished with faded chintz sofas and armchairs, occasional tables and bookcases. A large gilt mirror hangs over the sitting room fireplace, and there are watercolours of the Mediterranean and hunting scenes and an ancestral portrait stained with turf smoke. Some of the furniture might once have been valuable. The frayed rugs, freighted home from Empire safaris and colonial expeditions, might also have once been precious, before the decades of cinders and stains and domestic pets got at them.

In the library he finds a piano. He lifts the cover from the keys and plays the opening bars of Beethoven's 'Sonata in D Major'. It needs tuning. Middle E flat is broken. He wanders from room to room, opening cupboards and drawers lined with old newspapers, lifting down books from the shelves. *The Trainer and Breeder's Guide to Spaniels*, *The Collected Works of Somerville and Ross*, a whole case of bound copies of *Punch* and *The Illustrated London News*.

He walks down the shallow wooden steps into the cavernous cold of the kitchen. Linoleum, a scrubbed pine table, a deep porcelain sink, pots and pans and an old range with a chipped enamel door.

The phone rings in the hall.

'You're there.'

'Yes, I am here.'

This is an edited extract from a longer work in progress.

Sean Hardie was born in 1947. He worked as a journalist for BBC TV for ten years before switching to comedy to produce and write for a number of political satire programmes, including *Not The Nine O'Clock News* and *Spitting Image*. As well as television scripts, he has written three published novels and five stage plays. He's married to the poet and novelist Kerry Hardie and lives in Skeoughvosteen, County Kilkenny.

Bounded in a Nutshell

Gaja Cenciarelli

The doctor gets home after nine o'clock. She has learned to hold her back straight, even when she is overwhelmed by exhaustion. From her consulting rooms on the Aventine to her apartment on Viale Europa, she has driven with her eyes fixed straight ahead, her hands clutching the steering wheel.

Back home, she switches on the light and turns it down. Suffused brightness spreads from recessed ceiling lights. She places her handbag on the broad, ice-coloured corner sofa. She throws her head back and does a full rotation of the neck, first clockwise, then anticlockwise. Breathes in deeply, eyes closed.

When she opens her eyes again she sees before her the French windows that occupy the entire wall, separating the living room from the terrace. Into her field of vision, from the left, comes the concert grand piano and, on the right, three original photographs in their frames.

She stands stiff under the water. She moves her hands quickly across her shoulders, her legs, her calves. She points the shower head on both of her breasts and on her stomach to rinse away the shower gel. She closes her eyes, tenses her muscles.

She lays down the shower head and opens the glass doors. She wraps herself in the thick cotton bathrobe, lets go of the deep breath that she has been holding until that moment, puts on her slippers and goes back into the living room.

She rests her face against the glass of the French windows. She has no desire to go out on the balcony; she takes a quick glance out, then turns around and looks at the middle photograph. A woman portrayed as half body, half river running between outcrops of rock. In the background, an evergreen forest and mountains. The woman is resting, she has an arm draped over herself. The other arm is raised up at an angle, touching her head. Her breasts are large and rounded. The raised finger of her right hand follows their contours, with the slight hint of a smile.

Bed means detachment from the body. Her pyjamas have no hands. The fabric brushes against her skin, innocently. Lying flat, she pulls the duvet right up under her chin, then slides her arms under the sheet, being very careful not to touch herself.

Next morning, the doctor is examining a clinical report card, identical to a hundred others. The hospital seems deserted. It is one of those moments in which silence wipes out the existence of other people. The doctor wonders where they are, what they're doing. She goes back to studying the report card in her hand. In the background, somebody is muttering in the corridor.

'I'm not sure it's the best thing... You know how she is,' Silvia says.

'Ask her all the same. You've said it to everyone. How will this make you look?'

'That's right, I did say it to everyone. Including Alberto.'

'But it's been over for a while,' Vittorio grumbles. 'And they never even screwed... You know what *the lady doctor* is like.' Vittorio pulls a contemptuous face.

Silvia thinks about it, her eyes lowered. She's holding a paper cup in her hand. The other hand is buried in the pocket of her white coat.

'Worst case, they'll ignore each other. You just tell her you've set up a dinner for your birthday, then stop worrying about it.'

'Dr Aloisi?'

Vittorio turns around.

'You've got to sign the discharge sheet for Carazzi.'

'I'll be along. Silvia, listen to me... Actually, you should do it right away.' Vittorio points his chin at something behind Silvia's back. The doctor is moving through the corridor, as she does through the whole of the hospital, as though she were afraid of contagion. Almost on tiptoe, holding her breath.

'I'm off. *Au revoir* and the best of luck.' He winks at Silvia.

'Off you go, off you go ...' Silvia throws the paper cup into the waste basket and squares up in front of the doctor.

'Oh, hi...' She hesitates.

'Good morning.'

The doctor is looking at her, screwing up her eyes.

'I just wanted to remind you, before you get away from me again, that the 25th of November...'

'I know. It's your birthday.'

'That's it, yes. The thing is, I've organised a dinner ... I mean an informal buffet at my place. There will be about fifteen of us. I'd be pleased if you could come along.'

The doctor looks around. She squeezes her chin between index finger and thumb.

'Listen, tell you what... Remind me the day before. Anyway, it's not for another week.'

On the word *week*, the doctor resumes her pacing.

Silvia stands still in the middle of the no-man's-land made up of hospital corridors.

The doctor slips on her white coat and ties her hair back in a tousled ponytail. She takes a deep breath before starting her round of visits, even if those bodies make no sense.

While she is looking at the X-rays of Antonella Grimaudo's hip – Antonella, forty-four years old, has cancer of the right breast and was operated on four years previously by a surgeon who managed to disfigure her – the doctor's mobile phone vibrates.

She picks up the phone, looks at the display, does not answer.

Antonella Grimaudo has a handsome, puffy face, blue eyes, blonde hair which is dyed and a bit too long, two ex-husbands and two children. All four of them are supported by her teaching job. She fingers her rosary beads from morning to night.

The doctor slips the cell phone back into her pocket. She finds the Grimaudo woman irritating. She tries not to look her in the eye because she cannot abide that everlasting expression of sweet idiocy.

The surgeon says, 'The operation was a success. We put in a plate. Tomorrow we'll have her out of bed. A few steps on crutches, a couple more days' rest and then we can ship her back home.'

The anaesthetist pouts, slouches against the wall of the corridor, shakes his head. Antonella Grimaudo is still zonked by the anaesthetic. Dozing.

'Better for her if she doesn't wake up,' says the doctor.

Her mobile phone stops vibrating.

The doctor passes the X-ray slides back to the surgeon. She feels she's being followed by the eager gaze of the patients, although she knows it's not really herself they're looking at. It's the corridor. Their closest horizon. Shortcut to *the outside*. Life going on. Proof that there will be movement again in the future, not just the gridlock of frozen time.

A patient whose name she no longer remembers – dead now, she had cancer, she was thirty years old – used to stare at her every time she left the room where she was confined.

Donatella had never enjoyed being looked at, sometimes not even in the eyes.

One day, as she moved towards the corridor, she had turned suddenly to catch — *what was her name?* — that patient of hers in that brazen pose. She had glared at the woman with hatred.

'Could you do me the favour of turning your eyes up to the ceiling whenever I'm leaving this room? Apart from anything else, it would feel more natural, and it might cost you less of an effort.'

The girl had lowered her eyelids.

'I'm sorry. I don't mean to be rude... It wasn't you I was looking at.'

'Really?' Her tone betrayed her vexation.

'It's the passageway, you see, the space outside the room. I never thought I'd get fixated on a passageway.'

The girl had smiled.

'When you think about it, there are only a few steps between you and me, but in that short distance there's a world of difference...'

So now I've got a philosopher for a patient, the doctor had thought, uncomfortably.

'I didn't mean to offend ... I'm sorry.'

'No need. Get some rest, now,' the doctor had snapped. Then she had turned and left the room, her body pierced by another person's desire.

She says goodbye to the surgeon and the anaesthetist and feels the mobile phone vibrating in her pocket.

'Doctor, we've had a call from Signora Capriati's niece. Said she's tried to reach you on your mobile phone.'

'I'm working. What did she want?'

'Signora Capriati has deteriorated… Her niece wanted to know if you could call to see them, this afternoon.'

'Deteriorated? The only thing worse than her current state would be to lapse into a coma.'

'Yes, well, it seems Signora Capriati is barely responding to stimuli.'

'Nothing I can do about that. Get them to admit her.'

'They say they'll be expecting you at whatever time …'

'Not a chance. After my hospital rounds I have to go and see Signora Spizzini, the politician's wife. I don't even know how long it will take; I'm already aware that it's going to be a complicated meeting. I'm sorry about Signora Capriati, but if her niece phones again tell her that there's nothing to be done for her now other than getting her in somewhere. Unless they want to organise the whole thing at home.'

'Remember tomorrow evening…'

'Is the 25th of November,' the doctor remarks without even raising her eyes from the clinical record cards that she is examining.

'You asked me to be your PostIt,' Silvia says, sitting in front of her in the nurses' station. 'Are you coming?'

'I'll make up my mind tomorrow. I don't even know where I'm going to be in a quarter of an hour.'

'In the hospital, at a guess,' Silvia replies, sharply.

The doctor's mobile phone rings. The display gives the surname: Capriati. She does not answer.

Silvia stands up.

'Wait. Close the window behind my back, please. It's freezing and the papers are blowing around. I wonder who suffers from heat in November,' she says with sarcasm.

Silvia goes behind her, turns the handle to close the window. *What a bitch*, she thinks. *So good at her job, and such a bitch. A woman like her would be out of place anywhere. I really hope she doesn't come.* She leaves the room.

The doctor pouts when her mobile phone springs to life again.

'What is it, Francesca?'

'I've had a call from Signora Capriati's niece. Her aunt died two hours ago.'

'Send her a telegram,' she says curtly. 'And now, please, unless it's a *real* emergency, I've got some work to do.'

When she gets home that evening, she is worn out.

Josette has made her an Indian meal, but her exhaustion is stronger than her hunger. She eats two spicy samosas and puts the rest in the fridge.

Deciding not to have a shower, she heaves a sigh of relief at the thought of not having to touch herself.

She takes off her clothes automatically, her eyes fixed on her pyjamas, and she slides into bed, flat-out, her arms well clear of her body. Legs spread apart.

Translated from the Italian by Cormac Ó Cuilleanáin.

Gaja Cenciarelli was born and lives in Rome. She has a degree in Anglo-Irish literature and works as a literary translator. She has written several short stories and four books: *Il cerchio* (2003), *Extra Omnes. L'infinita scomparsa di Emanuela Orlandi* (2006), *Sangue del suo sangue* (2011), and *Roma. Tutto maiuscolo come sulle vecchie targhe* (2015). She is in the process of writing her fifth book, which will be published soon.

A Different Skin

Afric McGlinchey

'Je est un autre'

— Arthur Rimbaud

I take four trains each way, through bleary light.
Hide from the city noise, inside my head,
where there's only silence, or the memory of her cello.
My blood's grown thick; my body moves more slowly.
That first day, some racist in a drive-by aimed an egg.
It hit my back. He chased the car, caught up
at the lights and threw a punch.
The stairwell to our bedsit reeks with piss.

The hall is crammed with bicycles.
Once, I cycled to the river, sat all day and stared.
Pebbles. Floating foliage. Strange fish.
He roared at me when I returned,
thought he'd have to have it dredged.
Holds me when I wail at night.

I miss my mother. He tells me
to pretend she's dead.

They come from everywhere, the others,
Colombia, Peru, Fiji, Senegal.
Today we look at colours. She gestures to the window,
but of course, the sky is rarely blue.
I'm an immigrant, she says, *like you.*
And this — she points to the screen, a southern ocean —
THIS, is blue. She tells us about blue movies,
how blue's also an emotion.

In Advanced, we talk about erosion,
cliffs giving way, landing in the sea.
When a foreign language percolates your own
until its idioms even permeate your dreams,
that's not just acquisition, but erosion too.
It's only when I follow the slow river,
and the first real sun of summer
kisses fire to its skin, that I remember.

L'esprit

Afric McGlinchey

That Paris day, those empty, August Sunday streets,
heat lifting arms to fall and slap against my hips,
crop top revealing – my centre, as you called it,
when you caught up with me,
scraping your cane like a blind man,
although it was a limp you had,
the hump of a dromedary, or poet.
Safe enough, and a café open.
The coffee tasted bitter but made me feel grown up.
You were ancient, forty at least.
I glanced down; a beat.
You heard my mind.
'I know what you look like,
without clothes. Your belly's exactly
the centre of gravity
I'm wanting.'
Another coffee, bony fingers curling round your cup.
My croissant, spilling flakes onto my plate.

I pour a coffee now. *Yes, I'll be your model.*
Though I'm no longer twenty-two,
and you're just an abstract,
hands gesturing as you gaze intently,
shape your vision into stone.
Okay then, let's face it. I was scared.
Now, staring out at rain,
fingers tapping, far from Paris, your intense
attention — never since have I been seen like that —
I plan to walk those streets again,
to L'École des Beaux-Arts, touch
sculptures, and be touched.
For now, we sit here, you and me,
and though you're just a figment, I can
just about make out your absent shape, fingers
wrapped around your cup; and smile at you,
glance out the window
as evening eases into night.

By the Lee, You Sat Down and Wept

Afric McGlinchey

You've brought your fallout to share
with strange company,
low-down in repeatable boots,

clattering across Blarney Street or Patrick's Quay,
embracing the noise, because there's violence
in the silence of memory.

And the price of an Irish stranger's kiss is a hex,
and the headphones of a private disco
pound the walls of your heart.

By dawn, you are incoherent
in a doorway,
still steeped in musk,

homesick for the red dirt and thorny shade,
the long track
you could walk blindfold,

those old pieces of everyday life,
a blue teapot, your wrap-around java print,
bitter-sweet granadilla on the tongue.

Light sharpens the shadow
of your cheekbone,
aching river.

Ghost of the Fisher Cat

Afric McGlinchey

How to describe the topography
of the imagination?
Let's start with that fish,

lying in the gutter,
brought up from the river,
the legend.

Phew, the whiff!
Go on, observe for yourself.
Silver and shining as a new metal grid.

Like fauna between glacial layers.
twilight need offer nothing
more than the power of suggestion —

result of a cat's watery skirmishes,
for example. So perfect,
it could almost be a feat of taxidermy.

And look! There she goes! The cat,
her sinuous spring, back into the shadows.
You didn't catch her?

Well, there are always losses
and gains, as with any
fishing expedition.

It requires a certain leap of your own,
to jump out of one world
and into another.

Don't stare. Let your eyes go soft,
the way an animal tracker does.
Soon, you will see.

Afric McGlinchey's poetry collection, *The Lucky Star of Hidden Things*, was published by Salmon Poetry. Her work has been translated into Spanish, Irish, Polish and Italian. Her awards include a Hennessy Emerging Poetry Award, the Northern Liberties Poetry Prize (USA), Poets Meet Politics Prize and a Faber Academy fellowship. She is currently Poet in Residence at the West Cork Arts Centre. She has been awarded a Cork County Council arts bursary to work towards her second collection, forthcoming in 2016. Afric splits her mind/time/energy between Ireland, where she was born, and Zimbabwe, where she was raised. www.africmcglinchey.com

Hong Kong Fishbowl
Francesca Melandri

On Friday nights, when the pub is soaked in smoke and bodies, and many elbows threaten to topple the overflowing glasses, we, the waitresses, have to be very swift. As Donna and I are tall, we are growing formidable biceps on our left arms. We hold the trays high above our heads, and with iron smiles of determination we fend off the crowds. But Myla is short, though full of exotic charm, and has no choice but to swim underwater.

She plunges with her heavy loads of drinks beneath the tide line of waving cigarettes and stray, menacing limbs. She waddles gracefully, a real bar-fish, holding her breath like a pearl diver, and then pops out from some mysterious depth, offering her catch of beers to just the right customer. She is a natural, no doubt.

She is also very good with words. On slower days, like Sunday afternoons, we even hold contests. We choose a long word, like astrometaphysical or cinematographable, and fill in lists of words that can be made out of those letters. Myla is from the Philippines, and I, also, am not a native English speaker. So very often, when lost for words, we seek help from the bar's menu. This being a very Olde British Pub in the heart of Hong Kong ('Mad Dogs' the name, no less), our lists of words often include pasty, ploughman's lunch and bangers. Not to mention truffle, which is, of course, a favourite – we jot it in whenever possible. I dream of a multisyllabic English word which includes all the letters of fish'n'chips. I haven't found it yet.

I don't drink beer. I actually don't know anything about beer. Just for the sake of professionalism I have learnt some basic concepts: bitter, draft, straight glass and pint. But I belong to a culture of wine and grapes. Seeing wine put in as a single entry on the list of spirits – which boasts detailed descriptions of beers and cocktails – with the only distinction between red and white, makes me shudder. *Le plaisir du boire*, these British expats don't know what it is.

Americans are the best tippers as everybody knows – they have been trained since early childhood. The Chinese are the worst. Whenever a group of Chinese businessmen (or, heaven forbid, businesswomen) enters the pub, we girls all pretend to be very, very busy. We serve other tables, wipe ashtrays – if we are really short of chores we start doing cutlery. Doing cutlery means neatly folding paper napkins around a fork and a spoon, a fork and a knife, or just a spoon. As a special request, we can also provide personalised combinations (two forks, a single knife or, for the wierdos, a spoon and a toothpick). There is an elaborate technique involved, and each of us has a distinctive style.

Mind you, the Chinese businessmen – and women – are extremely polite, don't doodle on menus and know quickly what to order. Their only drawback is when they insist on having 'something with chicken'. They are not satisfied with our only poultry item, chicken liver paté – it doesn't look like chicken. Otherwise, serving them is pleasantly efficient. But tips – forget them.

But when Americans walk in we sprint.

'I go!' we all shout, and often it's nothing less than a race. We smile, pull back our curls, walk jauntily towards them. It's the real pros like Myla who, unless really busy at some other table, get to them first. The new, inexperienced ones, like Linda and I, more often than not are left behind – to cutlery. It's fair enough, I guess; experience stakes its claims.

But Myla and Donna and all the old hands were busy elsewhere last night, and I was the one, for once, to get the big catch. Three Texan sailors on leave: a waitress's dream come true. Moreover, they were sailing back home after the Gulf War. There's no better time to empty one's pockets than the homecoming after fighting – and I was there, ready to take their orders.

They asked me where I come from, like everybody always does. Like with everybody else, I chirped, 'Guess!' I didn't leave them time to answer and moved off swiftly with their orders to the bar. It's an old trick.

As I am not short or dark, my armpits are shaved and there is no hint of a moustache on my upper lip, nobody thinks I am Italian. Clichés are diehards – in Hong Kong, perhaps, more than anywhere else. When customers try to guess, they always start from way up north. (The sun of Thailand has bleached my hair.)

Some nights ago, a drunken Scot yelled at me, 'You must be from Reykyavik, Iceland!'

'No, I am from Rome, Italy!' I yelled back. We had to shout, because it was a very loud night – nothing personal. He shook his head, as if in a private sorrow.

'The world is changing,' he groaned.

When I came back to the sailors with their beers, they told me the results of their debate.

'You are Polish,' exclaimed the bald one with the nose of a bird of prey and sinewy shoulders.

'Maybe you are Swiss?' said the younger one, timidly.

'I am sure you are not Chinese,' said the thoughtful one with glasses.

As usual, the news that I'm Italian was greeted by loud astonished 'Wow!'s. I could see from their grins that this was an unexpected plus. I've a feeling that an Italian waitress in Hong Kong is rare enough to be considered wildly exotic, and promisingly sexy, whatever she looks like.

At one my shift was over. I stripped off the uniform and changed back into my clothes. The three guys were waiting to buy me drinks. They told me about the war they won but didn't fight in. They were talking all at once. 'We got there when the show was over.' I could see they were disappointed.

'But then, even the guys who did fight didn't have much fun.'

'It was just pushing buttons and watching videos.'

'It was a clean job,' said the one with spectacles.

'Too clean for me,' said Big Bald Eagle.

A thin wall of silence cut us off from the noisy bar. 'Well,' I said, 'some 100,000 people seem to have died...'

'Oh, those don't count,' answered the younger one, softly. 'They were just soldiers.'

Francesca Melandri, born in Rome in 1964, has written dozens of popular fiction shows for Italian television for more than two decades before debuting in literature with *Eva dorme* (Eva Sleeps) (2010), which has been translated into numerous European languages and won several Italian and European awards, including the Prix Européen des Lecteurs. Her second novel, *Più alto del mare* (*Higher than the Sea*) was shortlisted for the Europese Literatuurprijs and awarded several prizes including Premio Selezione Campiello. Her latest documentary film, *Vera* (2010), was in the official selection of many international festivals, including IDFAmsterdam and Full Frame in North Carolina, winning several prizes. She is currently at work on her third novel. She has a son and a daughter.

Liverpool/Lampedusa

Liz McManus

In the summer of 1850, Father Hore gave a sermon in Kilaveny church. He came from Coldblow in the parish of Our Lady's Island and was a stranger to our village, but his reputation had travelled before him. On that Sunday, people came from far and wide to hear him preach. A police spy in our midst said later that he had counted two thousand souls in all. Such a crowd pressed into the church that I feared I would not hear a word and yet, when Father Hore spoke, his voice was strong and true, ringing like a bell in the rafters.

He began by telling us why he intended to leave our ill-fated country, which was scourged by hunger and desolation. Then he asked each one of us in the congregation to join him on his journey to America.

'It is a new world,' he said, 'where land is free, there is no rent to pay ... and there every man may worship his God in the form he likes without incurring the ill-will of his fellow man, as is unfortunately too often the case here where man makes God and His Scripture the causes of ill-will and hatred instead of love.'*

I pondered on his words. It was true that we lived in the grip of a great disaster. The sweet stench of blight prevailed; the tilled fields around Shillelagh having blackened and died for yet another year. There were reports of famine everywhere. With my own eyes I witnessed a woman lying dead on the roadside, her mouth stained green with grass. My heart filled with sorrow at the sight. A year before, my sweet wife had died in childbirth and I had been left alone with my only surviving son. Dead mother, dead infant: God's will be done.

There were many who depended on the potato and were starving. I was fortunate: the crop of barley growing in my field meant that we had food on the table. How long, I wondered, would it last? Calamity makes a coward of any man; I was fearful that there would be no end to the disease and death piling up in the four corners of Ireland.

I had a choice and yet it was no choice at all. I sold my belongings and set out to follow the priest. Our destination is the state of Iowa, he told us. It sounded like the refrain of a song: *I-o-wa*... Firstly, he told us, we must board a ferry for Liverpool, where a ship awaits to take us across the ocean.

Thus, in the month of October, I stood on a ferry deck, surrounded by men from the parish who had chosen, like me, to put their trust in God and Father Hore. As we watched the Wicklow Mountains slip below the horizon

* From *A Farewell to Famine* by Jim Rees (Arklow Enterprise Centre, 1994).

– our last sight of home – my little boy shouted out in excitement.

Grief caught me by the throat and I turned away for fear of weeping.

Such a town as Liverpool I had never seen. Full of noise, mire and grandeur, it was populated by scoundrels and thieves. On every street they lay in wait to trick and rob an innocent traveller. When we came upon the docks we stopped in wonder at the sight of so many sailing ships and steamers abroad on the great river, but, driven by a dread of those lurking in the dark corners and alleyways, we did not linger. Like the Good Shepherd himself, Father Hore led us on through the streets to the boarding house of his friend, Mr Sable, an honest man, I was relieved to find, among all the villains.

That evening when we sat down to dinner our thoughts were already fixed on the prospect ahead. Somewhere, in the darkness, a ship, the *Ticonderoga*, was moored in Prince's Dock, relieved of the bales of cotton, barrels of flour and 9,000 staves that it had borne all the way from America. On the following day, a fresh consignment would be loaded: hundreds of men, women and children who were ready – as ready as anybody could be – to begin the journey westward to New Orleans.

We were a melancholy gathering until the door to the dining room opened and a man in sailor's garb entered. We could tell by his accent that he was a foreigner. Merry-eyed and swarthy, as gnarled and bent as the cork tree growing in Shillelagh graveyard, he had a way of gesticulating when he spoke that we found comical. He was from Rome, he announced, where His Holy Father the Pope lived. After a life at sea to which he was accustomed, he said, walking on land made him unsteady. For my own part, I thought the wine that he drank in copious amounts was the more likely cause.

Any distraction from our private thoughts was welcome and we cheerfully made room at the table for the stranger. What food was still uneaten we shared with him. In turn, to our delight, the sailor regaled us with many tales: of sunken treasures, sea monsters and a beautiful maiden he had once seen who had the tail of a fish. When the plates were cleared and the night drew in, he fell silent and became downcast. He even wept awhile and his tears only ceased when we filled up his mug with wine again.

We begged him to continue. Eventually he acquiesced, but when he spoke, his tone was grave and the stories he told us made my blood run cold: of shiploads of poor emigrants whose lives were lost out on the Atlantic ocean or the Mediterranean sea; of boats wrecked in storms off the island of Lampedusa.

That night, as I slept, my wife came to me. Or so I imagined.

In my dream a crowd of emigrants, my wife among them, huddled together on the deck of a boat. In the distance, high, murderous cliffs reared up out of the glittering sea. It was clear that the boat was drifting into danger. I shouted out a warning, but the only sound was the suck of waves scudding to the horizon.

Darkness was falling and lights twinkled out along the top of the cliffs. The boat, laden with passengers, started to twist and turn in the waves crashing against the rocks below. In a frantic attempt to attract attention, someone set fire to a blanket on deck. The spread of smoke and flames sent the passengers running towards the side of the vessel. The boat swayed, tipped over and sank, the waves engulfing its cargo. In my dream I heard the screams of men and women, I saw their mouths fill with water, their arms beseech the sky but I cared for only two: my beloved wife and my infant. As they sank into the depths, the umbilical cord still bound them, its coil and snarl adrift like weed. At the beginning of life, the imminence of death.

In the moment before drowning, the woman turned her face towards me and I realised that I was mistaken. She was not my wife. She was a stranger and unlike any woman that I had ever seen before: her skin was as black as coal, her cheeks pocked and scarred, her eyes were fathomless pools and a cloud of wild hair sprang around her head. As the waves closed in, the sound of her voice ruptured the night air. One word she cried out: *Lampedusa.*

I wake to the sound of my son weeping beside me in the bed. The hush of night and his childish cry upend time and location so completely in my mind that I am back, once more, in the old house beside Kilaveny Church. Gently, I take him in my arms and rock him until he sinks into a slumber. I close my eyes and try to sleep but sleep eludes me. In the attic room of a Liverpool boarding house, I lie awake, waiting for a new day to dawn. My only thought is to utter a prayer for her: the woman in my dream who is not my wife. Let us all be one, I pray, whether we perish on our voyage or live to tell the tale.

Liz McManus is a novelist and short fiction writer. Her awards include a Listowel award, the Irish PEN award and the Hennessy Award for New Irish Writing. Her first novel, *Acts of Subversion*, was shortlisted for the Aer Lingus/*Irish Times* Award. A parliamentarian for nineteen years, she was Minister for State for Housing and Urban Renewal in the Rainbow Government 1994-97. Her second novel, *A Shadow in the Yard*, was published in 2015. Currently she is Chairperson of the Board of the Irish Writers Centre.

The Ship
Giulio Mozzi

The guy from the suppliers turned up at one, as I was about to put the food on the table. I opened up, showed him the way, left him to get on with it. In a quarter of an hour he dismantled the bed, loaded it into his van and drove away. Meanwhile, my father and I were eating. Rice soup with parsley, yesterday's roast reheated, a mixed salad, some fruit.

I washed the plates.

That's when I went into the room and put everything back as it was before. I dragged the big chest of drawers over to the wall where the bed had been. I pulled the double bed back into the centre of the room. We had pushed it up against the wall with the window two years ago.

The room seems empty to me.

In the trolley we got in Ikea, all the stuff is still there: rubberised sheets, the package of incontinence pads, moistened wipes, toilet paper, ointments. We've got to do something about this stuff.

I filled two paper bags with leftover medicines. I'll bring them around to the local GP. As agreed.

These nights I've been waking up a lot: two o'clock, three o'clock, four o'clock. Just like the last two years, all those nights I slept with my family: Monday to Friday.

But last night I slept six hours on the trot. Woke up, stunned, at five o'clock. I started working: reading, writing.

If I didn't have the strange type of job that I do – I can do almost all of it in any place, at any time of the day or night, so long as I have my PC to hand – I don't know how I would have managed.

The days seem empty to me.

A friend who lives in Spain, a few months ago, warned me against what they call 'carer stress' or 'helper syndrome' – *síndrome del cuidador*. She sent me a link to an educational website.

Carer stress, according to this Spanish article, is a disorder found in people who carry out the role of main carer to a dependent person. It is characterised by physical and psychological burnout. The person is suddenly faced with a new situation, for which he or she has received no training, and which takes up all of his or her time and energy. The syndrome is believed to be produced by ongoing stress (not by an immediate short-term situation) in an everyday struggle against illness, which can wear out the carer's physical and mental reserves.

Trastorno is the Spanish for disorder. I liked that word. Another word I found disturbing: *agotamiento*, meaning burnout.

As for the symptoms, I had the lot. Jealousy towards my siblings, for example, mingled with resentment on account of their smaller commitment or their lesser ability in coping with everyday requirements: cleaning, changing, feeding.

I've always derived satisfaction from *doing a good job*. Cleaning and changing my mother was a fine case of a *job to be done well*: carefully, so as not to hurt her; quickly, so as not to tire her out too much; tactfully, so that she could accept what was happening; precisely and properly, to avoid rashes or infections. And nobody at all could do this job as well as I did: not even Mrs M, although it's her chosen line of work – this being the work that people from her country do in Italy – and she had taught me all about it.

The truth is, my siblings did everything they could, nothing less. They kept their lives on track, and those of their wives and husbands and children. The fact is, people have different limits, according to the different shape of each person's life. I'd felt much more alone than I really was.

I must ask forgiveness.

'It's not normal to see a man, a son, doing these things,' Mrs M used to say to me in the early days.

'Either I do this, or I hand my mother over to you twenty-four hours a day,' I used to reply. 'And you can't do twenty-four hours a day.'

In the beginning, though, I could see that she too was a bit jealous. Or maybe she was afraid that I, as a male, would not be capable of learning to do those things. That I'd be disgusted by them.

As far as I can make out, nothing disgusts me. I didn't know that before.

Maybe we could have done things differently. I liked feeding my mother. Preparing meals specially for her – they had to be easy to chew, easy to swallow – and trying to make something tasty, something that would make her want to eat, something that would help to counteract the current bouts of constipation or diarrhoea.

Spoon-feeding her. Brushing her teeth. Putting in her dentures, taking them out. Putting the dentures in a glass in the evening, in water with an effervescent tablet.

Maybe we could have done things differently: maybe we could have encouraged her small remaining areas of independence. Taken *less care* of her. Allowed her to spatter herself as she held the spoon in her hands misshapen by arthritis. That seemed to us a form of humiliation.

Mrs M is not an easy character. In recent days I've watched her wandering around the house. Not knowing what to do with herself. Every now and then she goes out for a breath of air; it looks as if she doesn't dare to go far. She stays out of the house for half an hour, an hour at most. Without my mother, there isn't much work. My father is still fairly independent. There are only a few things to be done, and in practice Mrs M doesn't even do those things.

Over the past two years, Mrs M and I have turned into a close-knit couple. After the confusion of the first few months, we gradually managed to divide up our tasks.

The ironing fell to her, shopping to me. Cooking was shared. She washed the body, I washed the hair. She covered evenings up to midnight, I was on duty from midnight to the next morning. She taught me, I learned from her.

I'm not an easy character either.

I have learned to be patient. Learned to cope with sudden outbursts of delirium, which can happen frequently during some periods. Learned that my mother was, among other things, a body, and that bodies have to be looked after. Learned to wake up and to fall asleep again. Learned how to interpret small signs: an outbreak of coughing, the colour of urine in the bag, a sudden change of mood.

I did not learn to tolerate my father. The very fact that I'm using the word *tolerate* says it all. Now I'm going to have to learn to take care of him, to give up thinking that, deep down, he's *fairly independent*.

I've learned to have conversations with my mother. To read her the newspaper. To listen to her telling tales from her childhood and youth. To tell her about A, my godson.

She only saw him once, a year ago, when he was eighteen months old. But she's heard about all his achievements. She got quite emotional when I showed her the video recording

— captured on the wing with a mobile phone — where he yells out his song: *The ship is sailing, oh yes it's sailing, but where it's going, nobody knows.*

In the tales she told from her childhood and youth, my mother used to include my siblings. My elder brother was present — already grown up — at her graduation ceremony. My sister was with her when, in those nights of 1943 or '44, the plane called Pippo was circling over her village and nobody ever knew whether it was reconnoitring, or heralding a bombing raid, or just about to swoop down and pepper them with a machine gun, randomly, in the dark.

My younger brother, in those tales, was always a small child. I was never there. Sometimes she was amazed that I couldn't remember, but she never managed to fit me into the scene.

The other evening, when I said goodbye to him at ten to ten — I had to run for the bus to reach my parents' home for the second half of the night — A said to me, as he often does when saying goodbye:

'You're going to see your mamma?'

'That's right.'

And I was off.

Once or twice a week I turn up with my PC, and we sit on the rug and look at the *movieses*, as he calls them. I'm amazed at how often, in children's films, there are mothers who disappear, mothers who die. *Bambi. Lucky* and *Zorba*. Or films with no mothers at all: *Pinocchio*. And then there are those terrifying figures that A calls *Fire-Eaters*. This goes for all of them: Cruella De Vil is a Fire-Eater.

That's why my favourite film of all is *The Aristocats*. Because the mother doesn't disappear, and the bad guy, Edgar the butler, is a laughable baddie, nothing special about him at all. Certainly not a Fire-Eater.

On the last day, a week ago, I wasn't there. I'd gone to teach my classes, far from home. My brother phoned from the hospital where they had rushed her the night before. I didn't stop my lesson at once. I finished the section I was talking about – it took ten minutes – and then I said: 'That's it for today.'

I ran for the train.

By the time I got to Padua, they had already put her in the fridge. My siblings had already spoken with the undertakers. Their estimate was on the kitchen table. Not having to handle that stuff was a relief.

I couldn't take any more.

A woman I know, a friend living far away, owns an undertaker's business. It's been in her family for two generations. She told me what they do, how they deal with bodies.

I didn't want to see her. I didn't attend the closing of the casket.

A few years ago I wrote a one-act play called *Emilio delle Tigri has Gone Away*. It was about the suicide of Emilio Salgari, the children's writer. In my play, Salgari shoots himself in his study (in real life, that's not what happened) and then, immediately after falling down, he gets up again. A disembodied voice starts to interrogate him, gives him the third degree. In order to die properly, to finish dying, the voice informs him, there's a certain procedure to be followed. Certain matters have to be clarified.

Meanwhile, everything goes on as normal. Salgari talks, he walks around his study. The only thing is, he can't leave that study. Outside the window the only thing to be seen is black; not a black sky, just plain black.

We never spoke about the afterlife, my mother and I. If I go into my parents' bedroom now, I see almost every trace of her wiped out. Within a few days the wipe-out will be complete.

Outside the window there's a blue sky, with little sparse white clouds.

Where the ship's going, nobody knows.

Translated from the Italian by Cormac Ó Cuilleanáin.

Giulio Mozzi was born in 1960, has written several books, and has not died yet.

Where the Wind Sleeps

Noel Monahan

Something will come to you in a dream that
Will help you find your way in abandoned places.
Here the wind sleeps with nettles and briars
In half-empty walls and the owl hatches
Her chicks in the belfry. Here apparitions
Of monks in off-white habits sleepwalk
Holding empty skulls in their hands and listening
To the slow noise
    Of old ways dying.
Each in his solitude finds dereliction,
Prayer that does not rest on words but lives
In the darkness and out of the depths of night
Heaven falls like snow on a linen altar,
Two candles burn, carnations as white as
Children's teeth are little nails of glory and grief.

Nuraghi Fields

Noel Monahan

i.m. Seamus Heaney

When they buried you in Belllaghy
I was somewhere else, out here
In Alghero, climbing the nuraghi fields
Where stones and more stones stand,
Life hardly changes, bushes bend
With the ways of the wind, sheep rest,
Tomatoes, figs are laid out to dry.
Up here with plants,
    animals and wind,
I picked blackberries in your honour,
Gave voice to the lines from the poem:
Each year I hoped they'd keep, knew they would not.
Down from the mountainside, I lit a candle
At La Chiesa della Misericordiae, dipped my finger
In the font of mercy.

Drumlins

Noel Monahan

When ice moved on at the end of an age,
Piles of stones stood naked, longing for grass.
The hills hand down root words, the people say.
Song of utterance, underworld of names:
Drumalee, Drumkerry, Drumamuck, Drumbo.
Ghostly ridges of calves, sheep, pigs and cows,
Story-book of hills, fields of fairy-tales
Cling like a last good-bye.
        I watch them sleep
Below a cloud, rivers flow, lakes rest.
A beauty all to themselves, no fine curves,
No straight lines, they linger like hermit huts,
Dropped, abandoned to an outspoken wind.
Hills too old for our clocks, they stand like
Unsent parcels waiting for ice to return.

Statue Park

Noel Monahan

After the wall came down, all statues of
The Communist Party were rounded up
From the streets of Budapest and taken
To a suburban garden to stand together:
Giant-sized pieces, Lenin in suit and
Waistcoat, stoic war and work heroes ...
Less at home now, they miss the busy squares,
Noisy cafés.
The garden sprouts a different shoot,
Some statues bloom and blush for shame,
Others smile like stand-up comics
Longing for a laugh. Tourists in Gucci sunglasses
Reflect on these symbols, Russian days
Behind a red brick wall. Outside, new houses
Breathe, windows open, night spills down the Danube.

Noel Monahan has published seven collections of poetry. His most recent collection, *Where The Wind Sleeps, New & Selected Poems*, was published by Salmon Poetry in May 2014. His literary awards include: the SeaCat National Award organised by Poetry Ireland, the Hiberno-English Poetry Award, and the Irish Writers' Union Poetry Award. In 2001 he won the P. J. O'Connor RTÉ Radio Drama Award for his play *Broken Cups* and in 2002 he was awarded The ASTI Achievements Award for his contribution to literature at home and abroad. *Celui Qui Porte Un Veau/ The Calf-Bearer*, a selection of his poetry, was published by Alidades in 2014.

Calamities

Ivano Porpora

I had a broken headlamp that wasn't lighting up the dawn and smoke clogging the cabin despite the early hour. I had enough oxygen for sixty seconds of life, same as I'd had for the last gazillion seconds — ever since my birth, forty years ago.

'I've been living for the last forty years with just one minute of life remaining,' I said. No reply. Forty years earlier I'd been a white pellet trapped in high-tension wires, and then I'd turned into light. By my side, another white pellet, but that one had turned grey and black; a brother who'd made up his mind that he'd never be my brother. And so I'd been stuck here on my own: long after the event, a pellet tangled in smoke trails, grimly intent on driving a car with a burnt-out headlamp. The road rushed towards us, sliced down the middle; the ditch lit up every now and then with a sideways leer. Scraps of grass were barely visible; the plain was still just a single stretch of marshland. Cloudy skies; the clouds a crude, unbroken tangle.

'Your face looks tired.'

'Didn't sleep much.'

Raffaele broke the crusty bread he'd bought just before calling to pick me up. He offered me a bit. 'Where are we today?'

'Turin. The Molinette hospital, then the trauma clinic.'

He nodded. He turned on the radio, started looking for traffic information among the morning programs. I glanced at the house of the woman I'd loved. You could see her roof from the highway; love sometimes becomes a delightful habit. 'One day I'll pass by this place and I'll look at the roof of your house,' I'd said to her.

Now we'd been looking at the back of a truck for nearly a quarter of an hour, swinging out its tail at every bend of the road. I was waiting for the moment when we would overtake, and I was thinking of how the day had gone so far, as the steel crossbeams stuck out dangerously from the trailer. Meanwhile, Raffaele was burning up his Marlboro Lights, bend after bend.

'You can die of those things.'

'You can die of anything. You can't measure life by death rates.'

'By what, then?'

'The number of times you step out of your comfort zone, on your own two feet. How many times have you stepped out?'

I said nothing.

'There you go.'

'And yourself?'

'Even less. Did you bring the samples?'

It was quite a thing, driving along against the backdrop of the black sky that was blackening more and more: it seemed as if the rain from the evening before, clogging the drains, had not been enough for us.

He was going over it all again. 'You had breakfast?'

'No.'

'How'd it go last night?'

'It went.'

'Manage to speak to her?'

I hesitated. 'No.'

'Drop me off at home,' I'd said to him the day before. He got it at once.

'Reconciliation dinner?' he asked. It was months since I'd come home so soon. As I'd got out of the car I'd looked at my workmate without saying a word; he had grinned at me, amused, then put the car into gear and disappeared into the traffic and the streets. My fingers were still feeling the strange touch of padded rubber from the dashboard. I'd stared at my hands, sniffed them. Coming into the house, I found bits of a shattered window on the living room floor. The stone was near the sideboard; I picked it up, felt the weight of it between my fingers. I sniffed that too, put it down on top of the radiator.

I'd set up dinner for two, with oysters, linguine (which got a bit overcooked), white wine. She turned up after a couple of hours, and everything was ready. She slid off her soaking raincoat with a half-smile. I had blown out the flame of my match an instant before she draped the coat over the drying rack.

'What's with the window?'

'Kids. I'll call the maintenance guy tomorrow.'

Later she told me about a colleague of hers at work who had burst into tears during a meeting. 'He was out of his head,' she said, detaching an oyster from its shell with her upper lip and sucking it.

'You like 'em?'

'They taste of the sea. He walked out, saying something about his wife. I think it's got to do with her having an affair. I don't know.'

Outside it was raining hard. We'd heard the raindrops hammering the windowsill, bouncing onto the floor where she'd put a floor cloth. After a few minutes, it was soaked through. We were speaking in whispers, as if the whole district could hear what we said. The light from the ceiling lamp threw strands of silver over her face.

We arrived at Molinette at eleven o'clock. The ward sister said they'd see us in the afternoon. We left the sample case on a chair in the waiting room. I looked at the creases in Raffaele's trousers. Then I looked outside. I went and fetched a couple of coffees from the automatic machine. Every now and then, he sent a message. We went and looked out the windows, at weird sunshine pushing through clouds.

'Look over there,' he said. Small boys were sculpting a woman out of sand at the bottom of a disused swimming pool. One of them was taking a video, sitting on a toilet which had somehow landed there, right in the middle, as the others were moulding the woman's shape: one did the thighs, one did the feet, one did the hair, one did the tits.

'Which of those would you like to be?' I asked him, pointing at the boys.

'Yourself?'

'I'd say the one doing the hair.'

He thought for a moment. 'I'd be the one who's taking the video,' he said.

'Why's that?'

'Because love's a thing that...' He didn't finish what he was saying. But Raffaele could never say complete sentences. He used to get stuck like that. I knew what was really on his mind: he always had the urge to get back to his garage and his woodwork, and every sentence he tried to speak got burned out by that consuming itch. The pieces he carved, I couldn't judge. They looked good to me. They all seemed like space turning in on itself – variations on a single theme.

'And last night, then?' he asked again.

'Did you notice they don't make films on *terrazze* any more?' she'd said to me the evening before.

'Well, *La Grande Bellezza* has plenty of *terrazze*.'

'No. Not like those ones. The ones from Italian films from the 1950s, the ones where they used to put clothes out to dry. My father used to take us looking at them, the *terrazze*.' She ate another oyster. 'He got us to walk between the clothes lines. He said you can judge a family by its laundry,' she continued.

'Hmm.'
'He was in floods of tears.'
'Your father?'
'My colleague at work.'

'What time are we going to be free?' Raffaele asked, and without waiting for an answer he opened the French windows leading out to the terrace and started smoking out there with a couple of nurses.

I didn't have the courage to tell her I'd set up the dinner to talk to her about an affair. I'd simply gone along with whatever she said. At the end of the dinner, a little tipsy, she'd asked me to make love with her – and it seemed unnatural to me that it should seem so natural. The day before, I'd been in Genoa, first at the Gaslini Hospital and then at a meeting for sales reps. I'd had sex with another woman, the rep who covered the Milan area. I'd had a long conversation with her the evening before, over a drink at the hotel bar. 'So your wife, now, you're unfaithful to her,' Raffaele said to me, after almost an hour of silence as we drove back. He wasn't smiling. To him, it was a statement of fact. This annoyed me. It seemed disrespectful. I couldn't explain to him that having sex with another woman was completely different from being unfaithful to your wife. At least that's what I'd thought as we were taking our clothes off. We'd done this very differently: I was quick and brazen, throwing my clothes wherever they fell; she was brazen and slow. I'd looked at my prick between my legs as though I were finding it again after many years: standing up, proud of its rediscovered identity. Between the body of this woman and the body of my wife I was surprised, however, to find no difference. They were two variations on a single theme.

'I'll call you,' I'd said to her as the lift came up to the landing, and she scowled without replying. I'd called my wife. From the road you could see the sea.

'How'd the course go?' she'd asked.

'Fifty fools who keep telling us over and over again how good they are, how strong they are, how motivated they are. Not one of them trying to look brighter than the rest.' As I said this I was thinking, 'I never realised she smells like that. It's a good smell.'

'And Raf?'

'He's here with me. Sends his best.'

'Give him my best. When you get back, will you wake me up?'

Next day, the world outside the windows was dark with clouds; a bird call was coming from close by. I couldn't see the bird. There were stale biscuits on the table. She'd already left for work. As I waited for Raffaele I thought over what he'd said.

'First time I was unfaithful to Erica, I went out on the road, for a walk. First thing I did. Years since I'd taken a walk around Boretto. Since I'd sniffed the air. And realised I was feeling like I'd felt when I lost my virginity. They could all see the change in me. Or so I thought. Everyone I passed. They knew I'd crossed the line that makes you a grown-up.' And he'd counted out, for my benefit, the list of the sacraments of this world: birth, first fight, first crush, first kiss, first fuck, first betrayal, and the death of the woman you love.

'Notice anything? Call themselves Christians, but every one of their sacraments is about themselves. At least the sacraments of this world are all related to other people.' He'd lit up a cigarette; I asked him to light me one too, and I'd started smoking, looking outside from time to time.

I'd told him I'd lain down on the bed with my arms thrown wide open, and surrendered to my lover as if she'd pointed a gun at my heart. We'd smoked a bit, drunk a bit; I'd told her I don't know much about wine.

'A man's got to know about wine. Definitely. And he's got to know how to hammer in a nail. Can you hammer in a nail?'

'Of course,' I'd told her. And it wasn't true.

She'd gone sulky. 'Know why I hate you?'

'No. Why?'

'Because up to last night I wasn't happy. And when you walk out the door I'll be unhappy. I need a steady kind of life.'

'You against change?'

'I just don't like calamities. Unless you've got a heart of stone, you can't get around those.'

She looked at me, ran her fingertips over my eyelids, closed one of them. When she took away her hand I lay there with one eye open, watching her as she got dressed again, trying to close the clasp of her bra. Her breasts filled the two cups perfectly. I was grateful to her for that. My open eye was the one that doesn't work as well as the other. If it had, her body would have stood out more clearly in my sight.

When I got back home, after dropping off Raffaele, I went walking around the nearby streets. I got the feeling I wasn't alone, that I had that brother of mine close at hand, smiling at my uncertainties as a man. Then I climbed the steps leading up to my apartment block, bumped into the doorkeeper and asked him if he knew a good glass fitter.

'She mentioned it to me, your wife, on her way out. Let's have a look,' he said. I went upstairs with him.

'What a mess. How did they...'

I showed him the stone. As I picked it up I was amazed once again by its consistency, by how perfect it was for the task assigned to it, after billions of years of being sanded down by water and the abrasions of wind. It seemed to me what the stone had done was exactly what it was meant to do, ever since the times when the waters that were one day to carry the Ark were lapping against it, when it was still a rough rock, and it seemed to me the place it was destined to land was right here, on my radiator, in my home.

And suddenly I felt affection for that stone.

Translated from the Italian by Cormac Ó Cuilleanáin.

Ivano Porpora was born and lives in Viadana, close to Mantova. He published *La conservazione metodica del dolore* (Einaudi) in 2012. He teaches writing in the evenings, so goes back home very, very late in the night. He is confident that his hard work is worth doing.

The Donor
Nuala Ní Chonchúir

The first time Xavier saw him he was startled that the boy looked nothing like him. *My son.* Xavier stood outside the school and gazed at him. No, there was not an ounce of him there. The boy looked like his mother: squat and quixotic. She – the mother – had a reality TV face; one of those faces that drips tears when her dough fails to prove, or her housemates vote her out.

'I was sure he would look like me,' Xavier complained to his sister Frances. 'Boys should look like their dads. The same way girls should never look like their dads. It's like a weird rule, you know?'

'But you're not his dad. Donors are not *dads*,' Frances said, shaking her plait to indicate annoyance, the same way she had since she was a girl.

The next time Xavier saw the child was after his first date with the boy's mother. *My son.* She was a noisy kisser. He didn't tell Frances that because, naturally, she would not approve. Frances was already angry with him for acting on the information she had provided from the clinic, where she was receptionist.

'It is not cool to stalk a kid outside his school. *Très* not cool,' Frances had said, from her splayed-out position on their father's sofa, where she and Xavier were enduring their filial Sunday visit.

'Why did you give me the file then? What did you think I was going to do?'

'I dunno. I thought you just wanted to read it.'

'It was you who got me into the whole thing in the first place,' Xavier said.

Frances shrugged in agreement and popped another liquorice allsort between her teeth.

'Got you into what thing?' their father asked, and they both ignored him.

The boy's mother's name was Mary, but she liked to be called Singhi since she had started to follow a guru.

'I'm on a fast path to enlightenment,' she told Xavier, over a curry in Vindaloo Tindaloo, and he nodded. After that it was all 'My guru this' and 'My guru that'. 'My guru centres my chakras,' or some such. Xavier wasn't really listening to what Singhi said; he was eyeing her mouth thinking, I *know* about you. He wanted to say aloud, 'I *know* about you.' And, 'You own my son.' *My son.* Why, he wondered, does a woman like this go and buy sperm? But he already knew why. She had an ozone-sized hole in her psyche, or her bliss, or some bloody place. A hole she tried to plug by various means, one of which was motherhood. It's as if she won the boy in a raffle, Xavier thought.

The kissing didn't start until after the dinner, until after they had bussed back to Singhi's house. They stood at her front door and Xavier knew his son was inside and he wanted to get in. So he kissed Singhi and she kissed him back, resonantly, sloppily, suckily. Jesus Christ, no wonder she had to resort to vials and petri dishes and the syringed swimmers of a stranger. *My son.*

'Do you want to come inside?' Singhi asked.

'Sure,' said Xavier, trying to tone down his delight in case she took the wrong meaning.

The sitting room was all scarves pinned to the walls, woven throws on the sofa and jangly light fittings. And it had a smell — something ripe and unpleasant. After the babysitter left, Xavier's son appeared at the bottom of the stairs, faux-sleepy, wearing *Mr Men* pyjama bottoms and nothing else. *My son.* The boy clearly wanted a look at his mother's visitor. Xavier gasped when he saw that the child's torso was identical to his own: pigeony and sallow. The boy's face, of course, was his mother's: big-lipped and — Xavier hated to think it — with a tilt that made him look unstable.

'Hello, little man,' Xavier said, wanting to anchor the boy to the room. The child looked to his mother for clues.

'Ludo,' she said, 'this is Xavier.'

Ludo? She could not be serious. 'Ludo,' Xavier said. 'That's a curious name. Playful.'

The boy smiled the same patronising grin that his mother wore. 'Ludo means "famous warrior",' the boy said, and slashed the air with an imaginary sword.

'Wow,' said Xavier, and he could already feel his interest in the child slipping, just as Frances had predicted.

'What the fuck are you doing this for?' Frances had said. 'You hate kids. I give you two months before you drop him.'

'Now,' Singhi said, clapping her hands. 'Up the wooden hill to Bedfordshire with you, Ludo. Xavier and I want to talk.' As she said this she winked and Xavier felt his bowels go slack.

The last time Xavier saw the child he studied him closely. Singhi had asked him to pick them up for a trip to the park. When she opened the door, a dog barrelled out of nowhere and flung itself at Xavier. He leapt to get out of its way.

'Jesus Christ!' Recovering himself, he said, 'Is that your dog?' to the boy. Xavier stared at Ludo; really, when you looked at him properly, there wasn't a trace of Xavier or Frances or their parents there, not a whit. *My son* ...

Ludo hunkered down and began to talk absolute shite to the mutt. 'Beauty! Beauty! Thassa girl, thassa girl. There-she-is. Yes, there-she-is. Wuh, wuh.' He let the dog lap his face and then tossed his head around like someone in love; Ludo even let it lick his mouth. Its name was Beauty, Xavier gathered, and decided not to mention that he couldn't stand dogs. He wasn't sure if there was meant to be irony in the dog's name; it was a grey, puggy thing

— mongrel from jaw to tail — and he truly had never seen an uglier mutt.

Ludo walked down the hallway, Beauty jumping crazily at his outstretched fingers, and Xavier shuffling behind. The house had that meaty, hairy stink that wraps itself inside your nostrils like a disease. This wasn't quite the bonding father-and-son encounter he had been hoping for.

'Meet Beauty,' Singhi said, smiling up at Xavier from the sofa, the dog between her legs, her fingernails scratching at its coat. Xavier whimpered a sort-of reply and looked at Singhi and Ludo. 'Beauty is not caused. It is. Did you know that, Xavier?'

'No, I can't say that I did.' He shoved his nose into his hand to escape the dog smell that crept like an aura around his head.

'Daddy gave Beauty to me,' Ludo said, and Xavier let his hand fall.

'Oh, really? Your daddy?'

'That's right,' Singhi said. 'She was a gift from Dieter.'

'Dieter?' Xavier squeaked.

'Dieter is Ludo's dad.' Seeing Xavier's expression, she pushed Beauty from her lap and stood in front of him. 'Oh, we're not together,' she said. 'Hey, you look a bit stressed out. Can I get you a chamomile tea?' Singhi cupped his elbows in her hands and pulled him towards her.

Xavier stepped back. 'You know, I'm not feeling great. I think I'd better go home and lie down, you know?'

'What about our trip to the park? Ludo's been so excited about it.'

'Another time, yeah?'

Xavier stumbled back along the corridor and let himself out the front door. He stood with his back to Singhi's house, his heart galloping in his chest. My son? he thought. *My* son? My *son*? *My son*?

Nuala Ní Chonchúir was born in Dublin and lives in East Galway. She has published four short story collections. The most recent, *Mother America*, appeared from New Island in 2012. Nuala's critically acclaimed second novel, *The Closet of Savage Mementos*, appeared in April 2014, also from New Island. In summer 2015, Penguin USA, Penguin Canada and Sandstone (UK) will publish Nuala's third novel, *Miss Emily*, about the poet Emily Dickinson and her Irish maid. www.nualanichonchuir.com

Mother Tongue

Federica Sgaggio

She looked into a dark window and saw herself all black, even the beige scarf knotted at her throat. She was wearing her rainproof jacket, the one for springtime.

She took a moment, pretending to glance at the slanting shelves, at a pair of very light silver-coloured sandals. Sandals. For a mythical summer.

To set the usual trap for herself, she took a small step to one side, placed her weight on one foot, and turned slightly to the right. Under her breast, a little further down, there was a curve, a slight curve. Too slight.

The rain was coming down on her in scattered, loose drops; she could not anticipate their rhythm. One landed on her eyelashes and caused her to close one eye. For the first time she realised that a drop is heavier when it slides down slowly.

She brought her eyes back to the window. How cold it was. That scratchy woollen beret she'd bought in Dingle, from that white-haired man she didn't like; a blonde curl...

Her legs were straight; the tightly fitting boots followed the outline of a shapely calf and wrapped themselves around her narrow ankles. But none of all this is any help to me, nothing's enough for me, she thought.

For a moment she looked at the shop window on the other side of the street, perhaps a phone shop, and then – without giving herself any advance warning, as the ritual required – she caught an outsider's glimpse of herself, reflected in the doors of Brown Thomas. There she is. A woman of about thirty, what a wonderful illusion. A profile, intersecting with the reflected profiles of other people, the shop assistants and the signs saying 'Don't Forget Mothers' Day', 'Experience the Extraordinary'.

This time she did succeed in surprising herself: she had never seen herself, up to now, with that youthful air of a bird of prey. A claw grasping life from the right side, gripping it where it doesn't hurt.

Before walking away again, she looked at the earpiece of the security man who – legs wide apart, hands grasped over his groin, clad in jacket, tie and black shirt – was scanning the hundreds of girls inside the shop who were all leaning towards something, tilted forward and held steady by a crowd that was itself slightly slanted. It must be one of those 'events'. Maybe a VIP or two: one of those actors with a Photoshop scowl, the rough magnetism of a cracked bowl filled with readymade soup; or maybe a fifteen-year-old blonde pop star already close to being destroyed by glamorous excess.

And given that two pairs of eyes, on meeting unexpectedly, can succeed in disclosing, in one unique moment, things about themselves they didn't even know they knew, it happened that when that man with his earpiece turned his eyes to lock on hers, she instantly recognised that he was at the Oscars ceremony, had once worked for the CIA, and was now on bodyguard duty for Cameron Diaz. He, on the other hand, understood that something was eating her up, that she was afraid of her body and her time, and that more than anything else she was scared of a man's hands, and each of them knew the other had got the message, knew that the things they'd gathered were true and weighty like the drops of that slow rainfall.

For a moment they were both frozen, caught out in the invisible thunder of each other's thoughts.

Then, she decided to seize the advantage that silence lent her, and started walking away again. *Men. Bastards.*

A little further along, on the left-hand side, was the café where Cormac G. Doherty, MRCPsych, had arranged to meet her.

All that cluster of consonants to say 'psychiatrist'. And they say Italian is a flowery language.

She had searched on the internet; she had read things, listened to a few podcasts, watched on YouTube an old speech that Cormac had given in Egypt at an international congress of other people also stuffed with consonants. A lovely speech about the ruined souls of those who have been children in a time of civil war. He spoke about the ceaseless movements of the eyes in a person who fears that every corner may hide an enemy. *Maybe I've been through my own civil war.*

She entered, pushing against the door with the weight of her body. She moved through a wall of hot, damp air, thick with the smell of coffee and the sickly sweet tang of fancy ingredients that get added to tart up the taste of enormous pastries.

She pulled off her beret, shook her head to free her hair, glanced out of the corner of one eye at her own reflection in the cut-glass mirror behind the counter. A man in a black apron, holding a tray in his hand, welcomed her with a gesture. She said hello to the air, walked past the 'Please Wait to be Seated' sign, and made for a free table, looking at the aproned man to see if the table might be all right for her. He nodded. The seats were padded but seemed uncomfortable. The little tables were dark, square. The corners of the plastic-coated menu were broken. She placed her handbag on the floor, took off her scarf and jacket. Sat down.

It was after lunch on an ordinary Thursday. Not that one could make out what lunchtime might be in this place. Anybody could eat anything at any time. On the streets, outside restaurants, there was the constant smell of butter and potatoes, some kind of vinegar, mustard, ketchup.

The big shopping rush had not yet come, but the café was already full. White dishes held monumental cakes and fortresses of whipped cream that settled in little dollops near mixed berries; or slices of salmon with a few salad leaves spotted with brown sauce. Proud to be Irish. She scanned the premises, playing her usual game. At least six Italians. It only took one detail, a colour, a posture. *Self-satisfied shits*. Ever since leaving Italy she could not abide their arrogant perfectionism.

She picked up the menu.

She placed her telephone on the table, looked at the display and saw that there had been one call from Cormac. She had had her iPhone in her pocket but she had not noticed it vibrating. She tried calling him back. Answering service. 'Hi, Cormac,' she said. 'I'm not in a hurry. Please take your time. It's hot in here.' *Warm, fuck it. The word is warm.* But it was too late now. Forget it.

She returned to the menu. Tea: no. Hot chocolate: no thanks. *That* watery, salty, chocolate drink: definitely not.

The man in the apron came over. On his lapel, a gilded badge gave his name as Juliusz.

'What will you have?' he asked.

'A coffee,' she replied.

'Espresso?' Spot the Italian: game of the day.

'No. Americano.'

'Anything else?'

'Hmm. I'll take a scone too.'

'With butter and jam?'

'Cream, please.'

Juliusz nodded and moved off.

She slipped her hand into her handbag and drew out a white envelope, one of those with a transparent panel.

She looked at it.

Inside the transparent panel was her name.

She opened the envelope. Her finger slid to lift up the flap; the sharp edge scored a tiny groove on the inside of her right thumb.

She raised her hand to her mouth and sucked the thin line of tiny spots of blood.

She took out a sheet of paper. In the last few hours she'd been through it five or six times, but she read it again.

The third line. She ran her eye across the row of dots to be sure that she was not following the wrong line. Over on the right was written '5.2'.

Not much. Numbers are the same in every language.

But when the coffee and scone came, she was thinking maybe it was enough.

No, not really, she said to herself. She put the envelope back in her bag. This time there were three of them, all first-class, but there's nothing left inside me all the same. Fair enough. I'm forty years old, so what? Okay, so I'm forty. And at the time of my civil war I was almost thirty-five. *Aha, so you want to keep it... And what sort of father would you be, may I ask? Stop snivelling! You and your notions of becoming the new Michelangelo. Tell me this: are we to spoon powdered marble into the feeding bottle? Think that's a good balanced diet, Maestro?*

The first sip of coffee seemed frightful to her, unbearable.

No, nothing to be done. I. Can't. Keep. The. Child. Of. A. Bastard. Like. You. Over and out.

That's how it should have gone, she thought.

Every time she imagined it, it got better and better.

The coffee burned the inside of her lips. She'd forgotten to ask in English, as she usually did, for 'half a cup, please, whatever the cup'. Nobody ever understood this. They asked if she would prefer a smaller cup, or an espresso, or hot water on the side. She could not bear hot drinks touching her too quickly. She wanted time, she needed a short pause that would let her prepare for the heat, the taste, the smell.

She wished she had been capable of humiliating him; that she could have been the one saying, *Sorry, sweetie, I'm in charge here and you're not in the frame.*

But no. He was the one, beautiful as a god, one of the better-looking gods, who had gazed into her eyes, pressed his big hands against her shoulders, guided her head onto his manly chest, kissed her on the neck and said four things to her: I have no job, you have no job, I don't know if you're the love of my life, it doesn't make sense having a child with you. She'd kept her eyes on the floor — a parquet floor, with long, honey-coloured wood blocks — as she asked him, 'But do you love me?' 'Yes,' he'd said. And then she thought one of those tragic things that every now and again she thought: no, that's enough, that's enough hands, I'm giving no more skin and flesh to any man, no man will ever again take anything of mine away from me.

The cream beside the scone was starting to turn liquid. The plate was flat and the fork was useless.

She wanted that cream even though she knew they made their cream buttery and sugarless because the devil hides in sugar whereas butter is manna sent by the Lord to the Chosen People of the Emerald Isle.

She looked at her index finger.

Yes, that's how.

She rubbed it along the bottom of the plate, pushing the cream forward. Like a tiny carpet, it gathered in wrinkly lines along the outer edge of her finger.

She brought the cream to her lips quickly, for fear it might run.

When Cormac came in, all hot and bothered, a pile of books under one arm and a big file of papers under the other, he sought her out with his eyes. He'd never seen her in his life. He was looking for the voice that had spoken with him on the phone, belonging to the woman who wanted to interview him for a story on post-traumatic stress syndrome. Maybe he too had tried a Google search. Who knows. A photo. Makes no difference. There were few photos of her on the web, actually.

She felt someone looking at her and raised her eyes.

When Cormac saw her for the first time, she had her finger in her mouth and was licking it.

And maybe it was on account of that finger that he told her the eyes from the Egypt conference were his, and she told him about when there were two of them and they gave her the anaesthetic and she woke up and was back to being one, and he told her that when his house was set on fire his mother was inside, and she asked him how have you managed to survive, and he told her he'd seen so many people die, and she said to him but I want life to come out of me, and he told her what colour a burnt woman turns, and she said that instead of a man she had chosen medical technology, and he said so many tears over a woman burnt to death, and she said that even technology had left her on her own and now she's scared, and he said don't be scared, and she looked at him and said I'm forty years old and not even Spanish donors are working, of course I'm scared, and he looked at her and said you'll be great, and she said thanks.

Maybe it was the finger that caused them to look at each other with eyes full of hunger and voices that touched.

And then they stood up.

They said *So long*.

Also, *See you soon*.

'So, we'll be in touch.'

'Yes, I'll let you know in a couple of days about those reports you asked for.'

'Bye, now.'

'Yes.'

A moment's silence.

Two.

'So, we'll talk soon, Cormac.'

'Yeah, I'll let you know.'

Standing there, stock still.

'Oh, actually, I've got to go to the Ladies,' she said.

'Actually, so have I. I mean, of course, the Gents,' he said, and smiled.

'So long, then,' she said.

'So long,' he said. 'See you soon, fellow spirit.'

He moved left. She moved right.

In there, everything was lined with black tiles.

Out of the row of toilet booths, she chose the one opposite the mirror.

She didn't look at herself on the way in, but on the way out she would be able to do it the moment she opened the door. Like that, to catch herself unawares, to see if she was beautiful and what light she had.

She went back up to the ground floor.

She went out onto the street.

The rain had stopped.

She did not set off at once.

Outside the door she had to pause.

She didn't know if he had already slipped away somewhere, left or right. He could still be inside, but she didn't look for him because she didn't want to see him again.

She had no room for anything except that long, curved thought that had suddenly sprung into her mind, filling it to the brim, arriving like a towering wave from another life: the thought that she didn't know how a *soul* could possess the kind of *affinity* that can be called *fellow spirit* in English; that when it came to forms of polite communication, an Italian woman – herself in particular – was utterly hopeless; that she didn't know whether two different languages have the same syntax of the senses; that she'd looked at no part of his body except his eyes; that she hadn't seen his hands and didn't know how they were shaped; that she couldn't remember how he was dressed, although maybe he was wearing a shirt; that she had not the slightest idea of how he occupied the space around himself; that the sweet smell of the food had swallowed the smell of him.

And that despite the littleness of all this – despite all this *nothingness* – she wanted him, on her. Wanted his weight, his heat.

Immediately after that – it only took a moment, and she was still standing there under that magnificent white grey blue black sky, now white again – she wondered if the same thing had happened to him; if something like that can happen to just one of two fellow spirits who have been close to one another, sucking in the space that separates one life from another, one country from another; the space that divides one man from one woman, the greatest distance of all. For such a long time she'd had nothing on her, besides her own skin. And she'd never had any part of another language on her.

A moment later she saw him. From the back, moving quickly. He must have come out without noticing her. She set off, walking behind him. He was going towards Wicklow Street. She had almost caught up with him and was about to say 'hey' but then she heard him say 'hi' and saw him lay his books and papers on the ground, and kiss a dark-haired, full-figured girl. She stopped. 'You don't think we're late?' she heard her asking. 'Not at all,' he replied, gathering up his stuff again. 'The ultrasound place is just around the corner. We've loads of time.'

His hands were small. Over his shirt he wore a blue outdoor jacket made of some crinkly material. He moved like the lord of the universe. Maybe he sprayed himself with Calvin Klein Eternity.

She went on her way and came to the windows of the COS store. The glass was too bright to see one's reflection, but she stared into it all the same. And thought, *Fellow spirits, my ass.*

Translated from the Italian by Cormac Ó Cuilleanáin.

Federica Sgaggio has published a couple of novels, some short stories and a well-received essay about journalism in Italy (*'Il paese dei buoni e dei cattivi'*). She worked as a journalist for quite a long time, then dived into a new life. She lived in Ireland for a while and knows she will be living there again soon.

Leaving the Island
William Wall

Then my sister Emily died. She fell from the watchtower. She was scrambling on the stones of the wall.

Jeannie said that Em had taken to following her, that she was always in and out of the tower.

Later the coroner would say that she had injured herself on the way down, that her back was broken too. Richard Wood and my father made the story straight for him. He praised their clear, concise evidence and expressed his sympathy with the family. A childhood accident, he said. He quoted the Bible. They know not what they do.

I was the one who found her. I should have been taking care of her. But I knew where to look. I brought her ashore. Richard Wood was not there. My mother waited at the pier. I carried Em to her and gave the child into her hands. Then I pushed the boat into deeper water and started the seagull engine. I went for the doctor and the lifeboat and I phoned Tiraneering from the public box above the pier. They got to the island before me.

My mother wanted to bury the child there but it was against the law.

Laws of interment are ancient instruments. They are designed to prevent contagion, disease and theft. They only *appear* to be concerned with dignity, love and hospitality. In reality a grave is a piece of property like any other. It is a small piece of land into which a child is put. It has a stone with the child's name. Time elapsed is recorded. It is a complete archive. It contains flesh and bone and memory and the parentheses of birth and death. And in the end, like most property, it is owned by someone other than the occupant. It is a mortgage on the past.

The coroner pieced together a narrative of her death for us.

We experienced it as a piece of fiction, less credible in fact because it had no internal order, no structuring principle. We fell apart. The world fell apart.

But the coroner's enquiry could not touch us.

My memories were useless and, in fact, I was already forgetting. It would take me thirty years to remember my part in it. I could tell how she slept with her nose to my back. How she held my mother's hand when she was talking to her, looking up at her face and just holding her hand like a toy. Those things cast no light on the matter, though he listened to them patiently enough.

My mother remembered. She gave evidence in a tight, hurt voice, like a frightened child reciting last night's homework. Even I could see that she was in danger of breaking, or that she was already broken and had been put together the wrong way. She kept looking at my father and he nodded and smiled at her.

This is what she said: Em had been with her in the kitchen. It was tea time. It was my day. Then Em was gone. Where is that notice box of a child? And where is Grace? I'll have to go after her. Then she broke down and cried. The coroner gave her tissues. He seemed to have a box ready just in case. Perhaps coroners always do.

In time she continued. She told them that she knew something terrible had happened.

Everyone looked for Em.

I was the one who saw her. I climbed the watchtower wall because it was the highest thing on the island. From the height of the tower I saw her drifting in the submarine currents, among the white and rounded shale from the last cliff fall. She wore blue dungarees and a pink and white striped shirt and one blue rubber dolly. Her hands were outstretched.

She sometimes slept like that too, face-down in her bed.

My mother's horror was terrible. I remember very little of it. There was a time when I recalled it all but I found it useless in dealing with her life or my own. Memory is an overrated capacity. It is most useful to those who need to deny things. I remember she was upstairs in bed and my sister Jeannie and I were sitting in the kitchen. There were night lights on the table because the electricity cable had failed, as it often did – boats were forever anchoring on it, despite the warning signs. My father and Richard Wood were upstairs. We could hear my mother's voice. It came in rapid stuttering bursts, like a sewing machine. I remember that an earwig walked across the table in front of us. Jeannie pinched it up and held it to the light. I saw its jaws working, its tail bending and straightening, its antennae. Then she dropped it into the night light. It fell into the molten wax and settled quickly down. It drowned. In the morning there was the shadow of the earwig in the cold wax.

My mother's horror was also perfectly reasonable. One of the things we forget is that the world itself is madder than anything our heads can make. How should one remember one's child falling into the sea? Sustaining injuries against the cliff on the way down? After that everything is impossible.

My mother's horror was all-encompassing, all-consuming. It devoured the night and the day, the sun and the moon, God and the future and everything in between. It paralysed us. It divided us.

Jeannie was crying too. I resented her for doing it. It seemed to me she wanted, as always, to be the centre of attention, but nobody paid her any heed. Her tearfulness turned into wailing and then I wanted to choke her. I slapped her once but it only made her worse. Shut up, I said, it's bad enough. Then I said, a pity it wasn't you.

Later, the night before we came out of the island – how long was it between Em's death and our crossing? – I woke to hear running and urgent voices. I stood on the bed to see out the window, but I could not see the ground. I ran down and saw that the front door was open. Richard had been sleeping on the kitchen floor. His sleeping bag was empty. I closed the door and went back to bed. My mother's room was empty too. It meant that she had run away again.

After a time I heard the voices coming back. Richard, my father, my mother. They did not go to bed. I fell asleep. In the morning Jeannie said she had been asleep all night, but I knew she hadn't been. She was listening too.

Where did my mother go that night? Nobody tells children these things. They hope, maybe they believe, that we sleep through every danger; that childhood is, in fact, a kind of sleepwalk through their adult world. Like someone said that madness is a nightmare in a waking world. And then later they assume we know. As if the simple act of growing up involves absorbing their memories into our own. All that time they were inventing the lie that would ravage my life. I could hear them talking it through. They were talking about me. If I had been older, stronger, wilder, I would have run away. I could swim ashore at high tide. It was the kind of thing I was good at. This is what you'll say to the guards, they told me, and this is what you'll say at the Coroner's Court. And then they told me a lie.

This is how we came out of the island. How the men on the lifeboat turned their backs out of natural sympathy. One of them was the fisherman who called to the house to tell his stories. He never looked at any of us. It was a wet day. They wore their long sou'westers, their sea boots. They were rough men. They made their living by farming or fishing but they volunteered to save people. They had seen madness before; the hills and the valleys were full of it. They did not want their eyes to say what they saw. They watched the sea and the boat and tended to it with skill and gentleness while my mother wept and raved and my father held her together and we children could not close our eyes.

This is an edited extract from Grace's Day, *a novel in progress.*

William Wall is the author of four novels, the most recent of which, *This Is The Country*, was long-listed for the 2005 Man Booker Prize; three collections of poetry and one of short fiction. His work has been translated into many languages and he translates from Italian. A longer version of this extract won the Virginia Faulkner Award.

My Man and Me

Gianpaolo Trevisi

My man and me, we met in the Virgin gym, or rather out-side it, because on that April afternoon five years ago we were the only two who didn't know the gym was closed that day, and we found ourselves outside the entrance with such a burning desire to do some running that ... that we got changed in our cars, as fast as only superheroes can, and then started running together along the length of the park, not far from our wonderful multi-tech gym. After just a few dozen metres of meadow, gravel and especially sky, we got the message: the park was much better than the gym. And we also realised that he and I had been stupid. We'd spent about ten months of arms brushing against each other, shy greetings and quick, curious glances, before introducing ourselves and sharing smiles and fears. At the end of every training session, which always took place at the same time on the same day, we'd hang our bathrobes on the question marks of our doubts and we'd take our shower, rinsing away even the very wish to know each other's names.

I go to the gym whenever I manage to get away from the private office of the managing director of a big company – a female managing director, actually – and the times I can escape with my bag on my shoulders, to go to the gym, are confined to the times when she's staging a little getaway of her own, taking a few hours out from her life.

She's a woman with sharp fingernails instead of eyes, and ten eyes instead of fingernails, but anyway, it's my belief that to work at the higher levels of finance one has to get one's organs confused with other objects, or simply swap them around: your face instead of your ass and vice versa, your wallet where your heart should be and your heart in a Louis Vuitton bag; and most importantly of all, a calculator where your brain should be and your brain lying open beside your desk, so that you can stuff it with sheets of paper and remember your appointments and phone calls. Apart from those little getaways, I worked beside this woman for at least twelve hours a day on quiet days, and twenty-four on busier days, which sometimes seem to be made up of forty-eight hours, when one considers that it's often necessary to do in any one hour twice the amount that it is humanly possible to achieve.

Starting from that run we began on that day of the mistake, my man and me, we've never stopped running together, even when we are walking or standing still and being taken over by dreams. I've never liked people who begin their conversations by saying 'my man' or 'my woman', because they give me the impression that they're trying to point to *their* object, *their* property and its boundaries, but in my case it's different. I talk about *my* man because I believe that there could only be one man with a heart like mine in the whole world, and he might have lived in Argentina, China, or the exact centre of the North Pole, instead of which he wakes up every morning with me, and he was standing beside me that day, in front of the gym entrance, reading the sign saying 'Closed', completing the other half of my own smile. He's my man, and that's all, and together we're so unique that we're often scared to show ourselves to the outside world.

With my lady-boss — that's what I like to call her — we often travel abroad and, depending on the country we're visiting, if there is something that's not working out, she beats me over the head in one of the four languages we share, so that everyone around can see that she's calling me to order and that she's demanding and implacable. When everything is going well, on the other hand, she is as sweet as an elder sister and showers me with smiles, gifts, leftovers from her enormous walk-in wardrobe, and when everything is truly perfect, she even rewards me with silence. I've been with her for years, and I never stop learning how she ticks and how she wants the work to be done, but maybe that's because she's constantly changing and never misses an opportunity to tell me that it would have been better to write something differently, or do something in another way.

For my man, and with my man, I keep looking for new escapades that we can plan, and any little scrap of time is enough to do this, whether it's at night, at dawn, or no time at all, just a few seconds to think about it and catch a whiff of his scent, as though he were standing beside me. We live together, and when the sky is full of stars we set up the tent on our terrace and sleep outside, waiting for one of those stars to come in and light up a thought, sliding on the silence; especially on Saturday evenings in the fine season, we sleep in the midst of geraniums, far from telephones, televisions, electric lights, alarm clocks; if anything is there with us it's nothing more than the music provided by our perfectly coloured soundtrack, by which I mean the 'Love Theme' by Ennio Morricone from *Cinema Paradiso*. My man works as a journalist, but he prefers to say that he writes; it could be a newspaper, a magazine, a piece of paper ripped from a copybook, a paper napkin or a leaf, but he just writes, and that's all there is to it, whereas I do nothing but read.

I know everything about my boss, almost everything; or rather, I know that every now and again she needs to disappear into the void. What happens inside that void is something I don't know and I don't even want to know, even if I can imagine, given that I always organise that void for her, in a different place every time, but always with the same person. This person is not her husband, and he's not one of the senior management team in her company. I book, I reserve, I pay, and I set up the lot: grand hotels, exclusive restaurants, weekends of busywork abroad, important documents to be signed near the seashore, endless all-night meetings. As for her husband, a lawyer who is so important and famous that he has forgotten about Justice and knows only the Law, I don't know if he suspects anything, or imagines it; but I certainly know what everybody knows, which is that he keeps the same strange timetables as his wife, has the same demanding weekend commitments, the same legal papers to be signed beside the sea, the same sudden nocturnal appointments, but this all works out very nicely. They have three children, two girls and a little boy; he was born on account of a virus that knocked out Mummy-and-Daddy's computer, both at the same time, and not being able to work or browse the internet they gave each other thirty minutes of what might almost be called love.

The little boy has a fabulous nanny and the girls are so stuffed with gifts, country house parties and love affairs straight from the glamour magazines that they never have time to reflect that they could be called Children of the Milan Stock Exchange rather than the offspring of their own parents; they are forever smiling and they have lovely long hair, usually plaited like the minute hands of clocks that twirl around faster than time.

My man and me, when we can manage, take our time and enjoy things little by little, as though we were sliding into an hourglass, as though time were a red wine to be sipped slowly by the fireside while it's cold and raining outside. The thing we like most, though, is going to the sea: not when we would be surrounded by beach umbrellas, deckchairs and suntan lotion – we stop at the start of the season and start once again when it ends; we rest on a wave that's tired of swimming, and we look down into the depths. It may happen that he's writing and I'm wandering around, it may happen that he's leaving as I arrive, but we start talking and we find each other in all of the countries where we haven't yet gone and perhaps never will, lands that don't exist and places that used to be. And when we come back we are tired, and we sway against the gentle wind to continue on our way.

My lady-boss, maintaining conditions of what only she believes to be the greatest secrecy, is 'seeing' another big boss, and the funny thing is that I often find myself contacting his secretary to plan their getaways properly. The other boss is the managing director of a big company and their liaison is going so well that they're considering a major merger that would turn the whole industrial scene upside down. The wife of the boss that my boss is seeing, I've heard it said – but nobody is really certain – is supposed to be seeing the head of legal affairs in our company, and many people say that this completes the picture perfectly, especially in view of the possible merger.

My man and me, we don't go out much with other people, and that's not because our friends, men, women, other couples, aren't always asking us out, although, to be honest, there may not be all that many of them. The fact is that our time seems to us to be so restricted that we're almost reluctant to share it with friends, to mix it into the chatter of other people. What we like doing is getting lost in the cinema, and when we go into those enormous multiscreen complexes, the moment one film ends we often head straight into another screen to see another film, until our eyes close and on the screen of our eyelids what we're watching is our own story. At the cinema it's rather like being beside the sea. Scene after scene, we travel, we fly, we love, we suffer and laugh, and we can even die, only to awake the moment the lights come up.

The thing that makes me smile the most, but which also gives me the greatest amount of work to do, is that I keep having to say one thing on the phone and then having to write the opposite in an email, or I have to print out a fake airline ticket for a boring destination and then swap the voucher for a warm romantic spot; it's tiring to stay late at the office and answer my phones and her phones, so that everyone will believe that she's in a meeting, whereas really she's off on a getaway. The day I was examined on my university thesis I didn't have this in mind, and when I thought about the word 'invent', I was thinking about making up plots and writing stories, rather than 'covering up' and 'pretending'.

My man and me, we read books together, by which I mean that we get into the exact centre of the bed and I read the left-hand page and he reads the right-hand one. It usually takes us months to finish a novel, and not because we're reading very little – quite the contrary – but because every two pages we start thinking about how a particular character appears to us, and we imagine the people and the stories so powerfully that after a while we can see them, sitting there beside us on the bed. In my opinion, I must say, it's nearly always those characters who switch off the lights and then get lost in the darkness, as we fall asleep with half a book each resting on our hearts.

My lady-boss manages to squeeze sport into her busy days, especially the ones that last forty-eight hours, and, in itself, this would not lead to any problems, except that she drags me into her sporting adventures too, with all the problems that leads to, because I hate golf, or rather I hate the world of golf, and another reason is that I wouldn't mind playing squash, but I wouldn't really want to lose every time, because if I don't she gets cross. I'm so accustomed to losing that the last time she didn't turn up, because she preferred a last-minute *get together*, I played against the wall and even then, inevitably, I lost.

My man and me, we play all the sports in the world and everything we do we manage to turn into a game, but the game we really love most of all is chasing madly after our kite in the middle of any old suburban meadow. Every day we add another metre to the line of the kite, in the hope that sooner or later, as it flies at night, it may reach such heights that it will link us to the moon, so that our fingers and eyes will be sprinkled with moon dust; maybe if we get to the moon we'd be able to love each other more in the light of the sun.

Now I'm at a lavish company dinner, at the end of which, immediately after the dessert and only after properly cleaning the table with silver brushes, we're supposed to sign the papers that tie up the most important merger of recent years. Present will be my lady-boss, her husband, the other boss, his wife, the head of legal affairs in our company, his girlfriend, the head of the legal department of the other company, and his wife, who up to recently – although many people say that in fact it never stopped – was carrying on an affair with the boss who sees my lady-boss; in one corner of the room, at a two-seater table, we can also see the six-year-old child born on account of the computer virus, his nanny, and a brand-new video game. In the opposite corner, but without any video games, the boss's secretary, her husband and myself are seated, ready to produce our bags, our papers, and our gold-plated pens. Of course my man had also been invited, but this evening he was forced to send the final draft of his exclusive story to his newspaper and couldn't even sacrifice one drop of his piratical Bic pen. All I can hear from the next table is numbers and calculations and statistics, and I can see the smiles that smile on one side only, and feet that play footsie on the other side, while thoughts, feigned loves, deceptions, getaways, fake meetings and masks made of clay and mud create such a level of confusion that all would be revealed if it were not for the shrieking of all those who are dying inside the video game of my lady-boss's son.

In the midst of all that hubbub, I lose myself in the depths of an empty glass, and I feel so out of place that I feel sick inside; I feel as if I'm in a swimsuit at the top of the world's highest mountain, or in a ski suit in mid-August, on the seashore. It seems that I'm in the wrong place, scandalously guilty of loving sincerely and without any lies and of not betraying my lover even with a glance. I manage to break free for a moment and rise to my feet, as though I were trying to hear more clearly the 'Love Theme' which, however, is not being wafted in from a nearby room, but from a thought within my own head.

I hide around the corner and one single desire fills my mind: to hear the voice of my man.

I call him on the phone and he answers on the first ring, as though he had been waiting there, and in the loudest voice, rising above all the noise in the world, I say to him: 'Hi, love, Matt here, just wanted to say, missing you like crazy.'

Translated from the Italian by Cormac Ó Cuilleanáin.

Gianpaolo Trevisi was born in Rome in 1969, to a father from Puglia a mother from Romagna and some moon dust they had touched the previous July. He was a Chief Superintendent in the National Police and graduated in Law, and he has been writing poetry, stories and novels for years. He has been living with his wife for a while now (she is much more beautiful than him), and two children who are his shining suns. Meanwhile, he keeps on dreaming.

Amanita

Fabio Viola

From the seats at the back, the heads of the bus passengers flare like matches. Each of those silken tangles sprouts up from the headrest in a fiery halo, exhaling cobalt fumes and melting into the vehicle's air conditioning like a nebula. In the middle I can see boiling plasma out of which, some-where far away, stars are being launched. Tiny particles of ice are floating, turquoise and emerald in colour. If I reach out a hand will I manage to brush against them? Capture them?

We're streaking along a road built of milk and marble, close to the fragile guardrail that separates us from a chasm hundreds of kilometres deep, with trees sprinkled along the wide country highway, pierced by rays of sunlight, casting grids of shadows, expanding and contracting, onto the bus windows.

Grandma had come to the bus stop with me, and had given me a farewell kiss on the forehead. Her long, long white hair was wrapped around my head in a blanket of smoke. 'And this is for the journey,' she'd said, slipping something into my pocket: a ball of transparent cling film. I'd closed my fist inside my coat until the bus was underway and my grandmother had disappeared behind the first bend in the road, after we'd left the town hall and its little piazza, with that surreal geometry straight out of M. C. Escher.

I'd got there a few days earlier, representing the family. Grandpa had died – or at least that's what was *insinuated* in Grandma's letter – and since nobody really wanted to spend three hours on the train, and two and half more on the bus, just to attend some pagan ritual in the woods, I was the one who got dispatched.

Given that I'd been unemployed for months – following an internship in the editorial offices of yet another newspaper which had gone bust after three months – it had been easy enough for my father to bribe me with a small contribution of four hundred euros, and my return tickets already printed. 'All you've got to do is show them when they ask you. You should be able to manage that.'

'Why don't you go?' I'd protested feebly. 'After all, he was your dad.'

'Here.' He'd shoved a couple of yellowish banknotes in my direction. 'You can buy a snack if there's a comfort break.'

On the train, I'd slept. At the station newsstand I'd bought the usual magazine for the journey (those men's magazines that are really for juveniles), but shortly after rolling it up to beat time to the music on my headphones,

I'd fallen asleep. The woman in the seat next to me tapped me on the leg. Pointing to the ticket I'd left in full view on the table top, she whispered, 'I think you should be getting off here.'

On the bus, I'd looked out on the mountainy landscape that we were entering. Parched hillsides, still strangely covered in vegetation, coloured in bright, grassy green and sprinkled with little clumps of conifers and shining white rocks, so bright as to seem like sun-struck windows.

My grandmother lived on the edge of a little village clinging to an outcrop of rock. It was stuck there like the membrane between the toes of a webbed foot. Pointing towards the sunset, when the rays of the sun lit it up sideways before sinking down behind the mountains, the village took on the consistency of gas. Opaque to the eyes, it seemed like a ghost behind a frosted glass window. At that time of day, the houses – all rebuilt with a provincial excess of effort and plasterwork – were encased in a layer of gold, translucent, reflecting sepia light onto the fields of the valley and giving the village a melancholy, fake-antique flavour.

When I got to my grandmother's house, my first greeting came not from her but from the dog. The old dog slunk up to me slowly, supple as a jaguar, clasping my legs in an affectionate embrace, but with slight hint of wariness, before slipping away across the grass and hiding behind the bushes in the garden. Suddenly, Grandma was standing before me, as if someone had superimposed her digitally on the scene.

'Did you see Amanita? Sixteen years old, and still amazing,' Grandma said, popping a kiss on my lips and stroking my face with her rough hands. 'And you, you're a splendid boy.'

From the outside it looked like a normal house in the Apennines – a close-knit pile of rocks resting on a lake of bright cement splotched with patches of damp – but inside, the main material was pinewood, as in a mountain hut. As many things as possible could trace their origins to timber: the furniture, the walls, the ceiling panels, even the kitchen receptacles – everything. The frames of the beds seemed to have sprouted from the floors. And rugs of all kinds – some thick Asiatic carpets in the living room, the usual Persian rugs in the corridors, woven psychedelic throws from the 1960s in both of the bedrooms, not to mention an obscene pink carpet in the bathroom. And then there was the tangle of tapestries on the walls.

'That one comes from Pathan,' Grandma said when she saw me lost in mindless speculation in front of the reddish twirls of the tapestry that dominated the living room. 'Your grandfather and me surrounded by gazelles, flamingos, wild donkeys, can you imagine? What a sight! We'd been to visit the Temple of Surya, an amazing old building dedicated to the sun god. We were knocked sideways by all that energy, but what really did it for us was the animals. Total ecstasy. When the guide, this adorable little boy from the neighbourhood who was missing two front teeth, one upper and one lower, told us it was time to go back to Dasada, we just took him by the hand. We looked into each other's eyes.

Ten, twenty minutes like that, and he got the message. We slept in the open. Your grandfather and I made love under the Indian stars.'

'With the guide right beside you?'

'Of course, even he knew that it was inevitable. There was this ... *thing*, you see, this love that flowed, swirled around us, you could reach out and touch it.' Grandma stroked the air with her hands and then shifted her long white hair from one shoulder to the other. 'I'll make you some tea. Jasmine?'

Later there was lunch: trout from the stream, aubergines and onions from the garden, a fruit salad of plums and persimmons — these too from the garden. All washed down with a white wine made by I don't know who, anyway a friend of hers there in the village. She called him 'my brother', and only spoke of him with her eyes closed.

'Don't you like fruit?' she asked, watching me dipping my spoon dubiously in the bowl. 'I put a sweet sauce on it, my speciality. Cane sugar, lemon, cardamom and cayenne. You sweat them in the pan for a couple of minutes, and use it to flavour whatever you like. I even put it on fish.'

'No, it's just I'm full up.'

'You'll have room for dessert, at least.' My grandmother had risen to her feet, knocking back a half-glass of white wine, and hurried into the kitchen. Amanita was staring at me with her big vacant eyes from the bamboo rocking chair where she had curled up.

'What breed is she, anyway?' I asked.

'In this house we don't talk about breeds, my dear. We all come from a single breed, a single spirit.'

'But she's a strange dog. She has a nose like a chihuahua, but bigger. And then there's her size, she's too big to be a chihuahua, plus she's black. Is she a mongrel?'

'I imagine she is. Like myself,' Grandma replied, cutting a slice of tart. From the place where she had cut, boiling vapour came out, accompanied by a strange vegetable smell. 'Like you.'

Amanita yawned. She must have heard that conversation about herself thousands of times.

'What's the tart made of?' I asked.

'It was your grandfather's favourite. All natural stuff.'

'But the ingredients?'

'All grown in our garden.' Grandma gave a sudden start and placed a hand on her heart, mouthing some silent words. 'All grown in *my* garden.'

I seized the opportunity to ask about Grandpa. 'But now... Where is he?'

'What, dear?'

'Grandpa. Where is...'

Grandma grasped my hand in hers – her free hand, as with the other one she was placing a smoking slice of tart on my plate. And she rubbed my palm with her thumb, slowly, but with a certain amount of force. 'He's inside here.'

'Yes, but I mean to say ... physically?'

'He's here, on Earth, where he's always been. In the universe.'

'Grandma, please, you know what I'm trying to say. Where is the *body*?' I said impatiently, and immediately felt sorry for saying that.

My grandmother looked at me, her eyes swollen with pity 'Eat up your tart now. It's nice and hot.'

'You sure?'

'Eat up, and then we'll talk about your grandfather.'

Grandma made a quick job of washing the dishes, using nothing but flowing water, then she joined me in the living room, where I was trying to get to know Amanita. Every attempt to stir the dog from her slumbers and engage her in play was failing.

'Amanita doesn't play games, my dear. She's not a child. She communicates.'

'Meaning?'

'Sometimes I stare into her eyes for hours. I get lost in there, I see faraway galaxies, planets, stars and quasars. In her eyes, I've seen the beginnings of the universe.'

'The Big Bang?'

My grandmother stifled a laugh. 'Call it what you like.'

'What do you call it?' I asked.

'The beginnings of the universe.' She smiled and again she took my hand in hers. 'I see you liked the tart.' Then she looked at Amanita and heaved a sigh. 'You see, my dear, she's on her own. Alone in the world. She doesn't know where her mother and father are, perhaps she can't even remember them. She's forced to live with us humans and she doesn't understand a single word we say. Her language is one that hasn't been corrupted by language. An undiluted code. My dear, imagine living in a world where nothing has a name. Even she has no name. She can't even think of the concept "I". She gets to meet her fellow creatures by chance when we wander and dance through the woods at night, and what do you think she can read in their eyes? What's all this? Where are we? Why am I here? No. Nothing. Can you understand how *alone* she is?'

'Yes, I think so...' In my world things had a name, but they didn't necessarily make sense.

'And yet that loneliness and nothingness are shining with love.'

'Um...'

My grandmother was disappointed by my lack of response. 'Tell me about your father, then. How is he?'

'As he always is. The usual.'

She sank onto the sofa with a sigh, then she closed her eyes and breathed slowly in, spreading her arms wide. When she blew the air out again she returned once more to staring at Amanita. She gestured to me, wanting me to move closer to the dog.

I felt an impulse to look into the dog's eyes. I got down on my hands and knees and advanced towards her. When my nose was close to hers, and I could feel the slight tickling of her bristles on my cheeks, I looked into those damp, dark eyes.

'Give her a hug, dear,' my grandmother said.

As I wrapped the dog in my arms, our eyes almost touching, my limbs grew light and I started to shake, as though rivers of magma were running through my bones. In the dense blackness of Amanita's eyes I began to clear a space for myself, between the reflections of her retina and minute dashes of coloured pigment. Kneeling in front of the dog, coiled up on the rocking chair, her grassy, hairy smell crept into my nostrils, sliding into some cavities of my brain. My legs were going soft.

'Grandma, what did you put in that tart?' I turned towards her. She was switching on the old record player – the one my father had given her when he moved over to compact discs. One of the last times that I'd seen her.

After a few moments of hissing, there was a slow sequence of plucked notes.

'That is the sound of the Koto, my dear. Let yourself go and look into the dog's eyes,' my grandmother said. Standing barefoot on a purple batik, she was embracing herself as she turned to the Indian tapestry. 'We're all alone in a cosmos that's growing ever colder, energy that's growing weaker with every pulse. The end of matter will be the end of time. Let's free ourselves from these pointless words.'

In the depths of Amanita's eyes, I was floating on the rings of Saturn among billions of particles of ice, passing through the geysers of Encelado, circling the clouds of Titan, and then setting out for a distant blue spot.

When terrestrial forms began to appear through the darkness – an Arab tapestry, a cuckoo clock – I found myself stretched on the purple batik in the living room. My grandmother was gently patting Amanita on the sofa, and smoking some kind of cigarette.

'Shall we go and see Grandfather?'

'I can't get up.' My body was nailed to the ground.

'Don't raise yourself up in the body, it's a waste of time. Use your mind.'

Grandma's garden was bounded by a hedge of thorns. Enclosed within that embrace was a series of small beds set aside for onions, tomatoes and other vegetables. Basil and rosemary plants scattered here and there decorated the scene. In the middle of the cultivated ground was a mound of fresh earth, of a strong brown colour and with vapours which were vaguely reminiscent of sewage. It was covered by a layer of petals from various flowers, most of them almost rotted away.

'It's Grandpa, isn't it?' I said when my body had finally caught up with my mind, which had been poring over this grave for who knows how long.

My grandmother put her arm around my shoulders and asked me to lie down with her. We stayed on the grass beside the mound for the whole afternoon, caressed by the wind. We observed the squirrels chasing each other around the oak trees. The comings and goings of insects on our skin.

My grandmother's 'brother' was a small, wine-soaked man, rather plump but low-sized, with hands tougher than wood, and more gnarled. When I introduced myself he greeted me cheerfully and shook my hand vigorously, then burst out laughing and threw his arms around me. Even his thinning hair gave off a powerful smell of wine. His head reached up as far as my chest. He had a deep voice, like a cow with a sore throat, but in any case, he did more laughing than speaking. A man of few words, every little phrase ended in explosions of gaiety which he followed up with great thumps on the back, both to me and to my grandmother.

Strolling around the garden that evening, a giant reefer in his mouth, with my grandmother following behind in a procession of exotic dance steps, he sketched his farewell ritual for my grandfather. He gestured here and there around the mound of earth, murmuring some inaudible phrases which always ended with the usual burst of laughter as he repeatedly scratched his crotch. Lastly, he handed his 'sister' a transparent bag, the ones used for preserving parsley in a freezer, which she immediately placed in her pocket with a rapturous sigh.

We dined on the leftovers of lunch. 'Sorry, my dear, this evening I'm really not up to cooking,' she apologised, patting me on the head. Amanita was asleep at the feet of her 'brother', whose name, I had gathered, was Altiero, and she was breathing quickly as though she were running.

'Who knows what she is dreaming,' I said, avoiding the cardamom sauce on the trout.

By way of response, Altiero just poured me more wine and my grandmother, knocking back her fifth glass in a single gulp, replied, 'She's travelling, my darling. She's not here right now.'

After the dessert, which this time I ate with a mixture of eagerness and suspicion, fearing what it might contain, my grandmother served walnut liqueur, homemade by Altiero. 'It's good stuff,' he said, thumping me on the back and bursting into laughter once again.

Then Grandma passed me two small earthy lumps and told me what had to be done. 'Eat one of them, and take a swallow of the walnut liqueur. Then eat another one.'

'But what sort of stuff is this?' I asked.

'Good stuff,' Altiero replied. More laughter.

'It's for the ritual,' my grandmother added. 'Calm down, dear.'

'What ritual are we talking about?' I asked. Suddenly I was missing the little room where I lived, my home as a thirty-year-old man. I thought longingly about the bored voices of my family, huddled around the television news in their drawing room.

'It's your grandfather's funeral. Isn't that why they sent you here?'

Maybe it was, that's what it was all about. But in my family I wasn't really *related* to anyone. I saw my uncles and aunts and cousins when necessary, I interacted with them for as long as it took, and they all vanished from my mind until the next meeting. There's something embarrassing about relations, almost more than the fact of having two parents and knowing how they made you, through biology, fluids and chemical reactions, rather than through a simple act of will. Relations are nobody in particular, you've chosen them even less, if that were possible, than you've chosen your mother and your father, and even though you share scraps of DNA there is nothing of *theirs*, really, within you. And yet these people talk as if they knew you, they give you advice when you don't ask for it, they pass judgement. You can even quarrel with them. I found it all too tiring, too embarrassing.

My grandmother began to tell the story of her trip to Siberia with my grandfather. The light in the room kept changing colours. 'This shaman, one of the Tunguso people, he was amazing. His time was split between his job in a bank in some horrible city over there, and his unending dialogue with the world of the dead. We were in this cave which I swear was *red*, red like fire, fighting your grandfather's illness. Your father must've told you about this. Or rather, your mother, as your father has a holy terror of diseases, and woe betide anyone who mentions them. Cities leave you scared stiff of words. Anyway, this shaman, wearing reindeer robes soaked with energy, shook his stick over your grandfather's chest. I swear, my dear, that *séance* was a perfect *kamlan'e*, a ceremony of matchless power. We literally *saw* the good spirits killing the evil ones as they swarmed up out of your grandfather's body. They were running them through with lances — maybe even burning lances, I don't remember. And meanwhile, the shaman was in a trance, and kept on repeating this formula that seemed like an alien language, a piercing litany that came from I don't know where inside him, certainly not from his throat.'

'Ah, who knows where it came from,' Altiero put in. Laughter.

'Don't be rude, little brother. My grandson doesn't know you,' Grandma said before joining in with an interminable burst of laughter of her own. Now I was following them – but was this possible? – through the garden, although I could not remember having got to my feet.

My grandmother kept on with her story. 'At this ritual there were very pretty girls, praying all around us as these spirits ... No, but really you should have been there, my dear. It's not a thing that can be expressed in words. And then indeed, your grandfather did get better. We threw his medicines into the river, we burned all the rubbish we had in the house and we made love on the ruins. Then we moved here. But you know all these stories already.'

As I was listening to my grandmother's account, I was glimpsing flashes of movement from the corner of my eye: Altiero doing something to the fire at my grandfather's grave. I could not turn towards him, though, my eyes being fixed on my grandmother who kept on talking and gesticulating while Amanita – I saw her arriving out of the other corner of my eye – sleepily joined us in the outdoors.

A moment later, while I was trying to suppress the image of my grandmother making love with my grandfather among the smoking ruins of her old apartment, I managed to turn towards Altiero and saw him naked, spreading mud on his chest. His penis was dangling soft and stubby amid the thick hair of his thighs, not quite long enough to cover his lurid, strangely hairless scrotum.

I averted my eyes from that swollen body and turned back to look at my grandmother, only to find her too half-naked, with breasts like vegetable marrows from which all the pulp has been sucked.

I too ended up naked – at some stage, I think it was Amanita's eyes that ordered me to get undressed – and then I attached myself to the slipstreams of light that followed Altiero and my grandmother wherever they went. They'd started trotting around the mound of earth. I swear the mound was *orange*-coloured, and throbbing. I followed in their wake until it became impossible to tell myself apart from that band of light within which my grandfather made his appearance, in a white tunic bordered in gold. He was swinging his arms around like a windmill and looked exactly like my father when young, I mean he looked exactly like me. My grandmother was stroking my neck, and murmuring words full of vowels.

The following morning I found myself wedged between Altiero and my grandmother on the big bed (the bed where my grandfather had died). I was the only one still naked. My spectacular erection made us appear like a chandelier that had fallen onto the mattress.

Altiero greeted me with laughter, and was still laughing when he made an appointment with my grandmother for the next day, to prune the roses. She told him she couldn't wait, and flung her arms passionately around him.

Later, after breakfasting on fruit and cardamom sauce, I went looking for Amanita, to say goodbye.

'She's not always around,' my grandmother told me. 'Amanita lives across many dimensions.'

Then we went down to the village and waited for the bus. I noticed that the few people who were out and about at that hour kept their distance from us.

'Your father's not the only one who avoids me,' Grandma said. 'But that's all right.'

Shortly after the bus got going, I sampled the treat that Grandma had given me. I chewed it slowly to find out what it tasted of. Earth, mostly.

Now the bus floats into the depot with a great swirl of coloured laser lights, as before my very eyes a flight of swans with humanoid heads, flying alongside, morphs into the shape of a railway station.

When the train gets going, against a fuzzy backdrop of mountains and a scalding stretch of houses and trees and lines of tar outside the windows marking our journey, we hold hands in the carriage and smile as we're catapulted at speed towards a tunnel. But we feel no fear of crashing against the dark. We know that darkness will absorb us into reflections like the light flecks in Amanita's eyes, and every molecule of every thing will be motionless, undefined and timeless, until an immense band of photons gathers us again and then everything will resume its old shape, matter will exist once more, and with matter, reality, and time, and the four hundred euros that my father transferred into my wretchedly thin current account.

One way or another, I get home. Standing outside our apartment, I send a text message to my father: *Not coming back. Staying on with Gran.*

He replies a few seconds later: *Saw you crossing the yard.*

At this point, I may as well go in.

Translated from the Italian by Cormac Ó Cuilleanáin.

Fabio Viola was born in Rome in 1975, lived in Osaka, Japan and now lives in Milan. He has published four novels, the latest being *I dirimpettai* (2015), longlisted for the Italian Strega Prize. He has translated Edmund White, Helen Humphreys and Mark Twain into Italian.